The Professor *of* Light

Also by Marina Budhos

House of Waiting

Remix: Conversations with
Immigrant Teenagers
(nonfiction)

The Professor
of Light

Marina Budhos

G. P. PUTNAM'S SONS   *New York*

This is a work of fiction. The events described are
imaginary, and the characters are fictitious and not
intended to represent specific living persons.

Copyright © 1999 by Marina Budhos

G. P. Putnam's Sons
Publishers Since 1838
a member of
Penguin Putnam Inc.
375 Hudson Street
New York, NY 10014

Portions of this book have appeared, in different form,
in *The Portable Lower East Side: New Asia*
and *The Caribbean Writer.*

The definition on the epigraph page is from the Random House
Webster's Pocket Dictionary, © 1995, 1997.

Library of Congress Cataloging-in-Publication Data

Budhos, Marina Tamar.
The professor of light / Marina Budhos.
p. cm.
ISBN 0-399-14473-0
1. Guyanese Americans—Fiction.   I. Title.
PS3552.U3476P76   1999   98-33904 CIP
813'.54—dc21

The text of this book is set in Walbaum MT.
Book design by Amanda Dewey

Printed in the United States of America
1   3   5   7   9   10   8   6   4   2

Profound gratitude to Robin Bradford, Johanna Keller, and Deborah Wolfe, my dear readers. Thanks to my delightful friends and family: Lisa Aronson, Sara Bershtel, Shirley Budhos, Menon Dwarka, Luis Francia, Peter Kaufman, Maricel Presilla, Ed Rothfarb, Kim Vaeth, Sarah Midori Zimmerman; and to my colleagues at Goddard College for their feisty and supportive community.

I am grateful to the Rona Jaffe Foundation for a grant that enabled me to finish this book, and to the Virginia Center for the Creative Arts and the MacDowell Colony.

It was in the stars that Henry Dunow would be the agent for this book. He was perfect—enthusiastic and funny in his own Henry-way. He led me to Faith Sale, the perfect editor, whose graceful and exacting touch made me push for more. Jennifer Carlson, Aimée Taub, and Anna Jardine kept track of matters big and small.

The true hero behind this book is my husband, Marc Aronson. From the moment we met, he has spurred me on, read countless drafts, and even slogged through the Guyana mud. He breathed love and life into every page, every day we've been together. Thank you.

To Marc

Light, n, adj

    —n 1. that which makes things visible or gives illumination. 2. daylight. 3. aspect. 4. enlightenment.

    —adj 5. not dark. 6. not heavy.

The Professor *of* Light

Summers

Summers we went to England.

Every May, my mother dragged the Samsonite luggage down from our attic and started packing. In flew the permanent-press dresses, the wool skirts and lamb's-wool sweaters she'd bought for herself the summer before. There were my clothes too: black rubber Wellingtons, since rain was always a threat; leather sandals with a punched design; polo shirts and navy shorts, for I insisted on dressing the same as my cousin George. Squeezed into the edges of the overstuffed suitcase were packages of sheets and pillowcases for my aunt, American denim jackets and dungarees for George and my younger cousin Timmy.

My father's suitcase smelled of leather and tobacco. He

smoked a pipe, and brought a zippered pouch with pipe cleaners, a summer's supply of cherry-wood tobacco, and six different pipes. His shirts, each one sheathed in a sky-blue ribbon from the Chinese laundry, were lined up stiffly on the bed like a row of headless soldiers, pockets tattooed with ink stains.

During the packing, my parents' bedroom was turned topsy-turvy; drawers gaped, dry-cleaning wrap lay wadded on the floor. Textbooks and papers from my father's study were spread about the bed, night tables, and carpet. "When are you going to organize this?" my mother would shout at him.

Running a hand through his rumpled gray hair, he would look at her in anguish, and say, "I'm trying, I'm really trying, Sonia."

The simplest of decisions confused my father. For hours while my mother packed, he paced and chewed on his pipe stem, scribbled notes on napkins, until, with a weary sigh, he settled onto the bed, next to the careful piles of clothes, with his face in his hands. Around and around his mulling went, all about physics and philosophy and mathematics, how to finish his book this summer, so that the question of what books and papers he should bring remained a damp, annoying mystery in his mind.

"Just tell me!" my mother would finally demand.

"I can't decide, Sonia," he would answer. "Put in whatever you want."

"That's an original idea," she would fume, and nevertheless fill one medium-sized suitcase with his belongings, sort his crumpled papers into manila folders, label them with a marker, and type a checklist of the books and articles he wanted to read that summer.

The Professor *of* Light

My father was a dreamer, a storyteller, a thinker. Always restless, he moved from mathematics to physics to philosophy. He had a fickleness of character, a terror of the finish line. For years, he'd been struggling to complete his book, an extraordinary opus that blended the various disciplines he had tramped through, and dared to resolve the particle–wave paradox of light.

At the college where he taught, he was the resident guru, sitting on his leather throne in his ferociously messy office. In half-sentences, he sketched for students the gloomy tunnels of belief and the well-lit corridors of rational thought. He showed a passion for both. His soft, rolling voice, echoing with Caribbean cadences and bits of Hindi, made a gentle, if troubled, truce between the two.

Sometimes I accompanied my father to the college, where I scurried to keep up with his long legs, his folder of papers tucked under my arm. My father was tall, with shiny brown skin and unruly silver hair atop a soft, youthful face. He moved in loose-limbed thrusts, as if he could not be bothered with the physical weight of his clothes.

One September day, when I was nine years old, he brought me to his History of Ideas class. I sat shyly on his desk, next to a stack of books, knocking my heels against the wooden side. "This here my daughter, Megan," he announced to the room of puzzled faces. "She's going to teach you a lot of things about philosophy."

The students stared and giggled.

"All right. I can see you think I'm joking. You know what my daughter asked me the other day? She asked, 'How did I think before I knew how to speak?' "

A boy snickered. "So what?"

"But it's an essential question." My father took off his jacket and wrote on the blackboard: *1 + 1 = ?*

The boy yelled out, "You gotta be kidding."

My father perched on the edge of the desk, eyes bright. "Now can anyone tell me, how much is one plus one?"

"What is this, remedial math?"

"Just answer the question."

The boy groaned out a "Two."

"You sure?"

"Of course I'm sure!"

"How do you know what two really is? Or do you know that a composite of one and one is two? There you go, my man, one of the most essential questions in philosophy, what my daughter asked about before: a priori knowledge."

As the boy's face fell, a triumphant fire glowed in me. A girl raised her hand. "Professor Singh, I'm confused. You told us to read *The Republic.*"

"Forget about the assignment. Tell me this: What is a philosopher?"

"Someone who asks dumb questions?" the boy who snickered before asked.

"Very good!" my father said. "Almost. That's my daughter, then. Meggie asks questions all the time. 'Where do I come from?' 'Why can't time move backward?' she asks. Why, why, why? She drives me crazy with all her questions!"

I smiled, delighted that my father had remembered what I said, and thought it important.

"She's not a philosopher," a girl with straight blond hair objected. "That's just curiosity."

"Even better!" my father exclaimed. "Plato tells us the very same thing. 'If curiosity makes a philosopher, you will find many a strange being will have a title to the name.' " He pulled a book out of the pile and tossed it lightly to the girl. "So why isn't my daughter here a philosopher?"

"Because she doesn't have answers?"

"Because she's too short?"

My father scooped up the rest of the books, carried them to the open window, and flung them outside. The class watched in amazement as the books took wing on the autumn breeze and settled on the grassy slope. Then my father drew the blinds shut.

"Imagine you are in a room like this, chained to your desk. The most you can see are shapes thrown against a wall from a distant fire, the shadows of trees as they move in the wind. For all you know, though, those shadows are the real trees.

"All of a sudden I open the blinds and now you can see the trees and the grass up on a little hill. You are very curious, like my daughter here, so you want to move closer to the fire, to the source of this new sensation. You climb out the window and start walking up the hill. Your eyes ache, you're not used to so much light. This is Plato's parable of the cave. The cave is the world of sight and the light of the fire is the sun. The journey upward is into the intellectual world."

I had shut my eyes. I had lost myself, my body, and was traveling in a boat in the night. My father had slipped into his Caribbean storytelling voice that lapped all around, sweet and soothing, as he coaxed me toward the distant, glimmering questions he lit up ahead.

"When I was a little boy in my short-short pants, I grew up in darkness. The only light I had was a kerosene lamp. I had nothing else but the wisdom of my father and mother. So I learned to read and ask questions that helped me journey to the truth.

"Now, our man Plato also learned from the wisdom of his forefathers, the pre-Socratics. He believed that every one of us has a fire in our eye that leads outward and joins with the light of the world. Think of our journey as a bridge of fire, gently swaying over a chasm of ignorance. Slowly, slowly, step by step, we walk along this bridge of fire, suspended in the air, into the grand radiance of knowledge."

My eyes opened and I realized my father was gripping me by the waist. I was hanging in the air. One of the students had pulled up the blinds to show a maintenance man picking up the books, one by one, from the slope outside. The other students' faces lifted with surprise. A warm pleasure trickled to my stomach. I knew they were jealous of me because I was his daughter and my life with him would be extraordinary.

Yet there was always his strange preoccupation that dragged us back into darkness and uncertainty. On the question of light my father remained stumped.

For years, he hung, like a frightened acrobat, in the balance between particle and wave. The rope could suddenly snap, and he might tumble down. Or perhaps it was he who contemplated snapping, and this frightened him. It also frightened me. For something was never quite right with my father.

But I am getting ahead of myself. Almost every night, my father told me stories, drew me into his questions, until I grew drowsy with sleep. His voice became a sound, the struck notes of a song, the start of the world as I was coming to know it.

This is a story about many things. It is about light. It is about a mixed-up family that came together every summer to pretend it was whole. It is about the tales of long before. And it is about a father who one day stopped talking.

And as with all stories, we must start at the beginning.

Long, long ago, a great ocean of milk spawned the universe, the stars were made of candied milk, the fields were bright with rice and sugar. Then the continents crashed into one another. A piece of the world, called England, banged into another part of the world, known as Hindustan. Many of the people fell out, like tiny dust motes. They scattered here and there, to China and Africa and the West Indies. Bharat Singh was one of those people.

On a sultry summer day Bharat was walking in his village in Bihar, when an Englishman came to him and told him of a land that was so rich the people there wore gold on their skins. He promised him work in fields far off, on the other side of the ocean.

The Professor of Light

Once on the boat that sailed from the Bay of Bengal, Bharat despaired at what he saw, men and women who did not bathe every day, who forgot the names of their gods. He tried not to lose himself in a blue ache of nothing. Every morning he kissed his amulet, sprinkled his feet with seven drops of water, and prayed for the harmony of his soul.

In British Guiana he discovered no gold. There were only fields and fields of sugar cane. He worked hard, planting and cutting cane on a big estate, marrying a girl who worked in a nearby rice mill, and who bore him five children, two boys and three girls. After many years, he was offered a plot of land to grow his own cane. The first season he did well enough to buy another plot and plant another crop. In this way, he hoped to make enough money to build a decent house for his family.

An Englishman with a high stiff collar drove up to his gate one day in a shiny automobile. The Englishman carried a mango for each one of Bharat's five children and said that Jesus loved these children like the fingers on his hand. The man told Bharat that if his children went to the church and school down the road, they could take an overseas exam and go to the great universities in England and America. Eventually they would come back and drive an automobile like his own and drink tea in china cups.

After that, every Sunday, Bharat sat on the bench of the Presbyterian church and sang to the new god that lived on top of the zinc roof. His sons Joseph and Warren went to the Presbyterian school and learned to comb the creole right out of their talk.

Bharat grew very afraid. He worried that his two sons would do better than he did, and leave him behind. When he built their new house, instead of summoning the pastor, he went to the temple pandits. They blessed the door and warned him, "Teach your children, yet break them well. Otherwise they will be lost to you."

The next afternoon, when his sons came home from school, Bharat dragged them to the boiling house. He grabbed the younger son's hand and plunged it into the hot molasses. Warren cried. He thought his fingers were melting and would soon fall off. Bharat pulled the boy's hand from the bubbling molasses, and a thin strand hung between his thumb and forefinger.

"This here is called striking," Bharat told him. "This is when molasses turn to sugar, and you got to quick put the flame down, or the sugar is no good.

"Your self is like this. It can be many things. Some of the time hot and molten. Other time hard and brittle. But you must never forget all I give you, all you come from."

Listen well, for this is your story too. You can take a little bit of each that has seeded you, so you can know who you are. For you are from the people who have spread scattershot throughout the world. You can never sit still, you are jumpy, like atoms flashing through space.

It is really a very long tale, written by many great men, each of whom had his own version. Remember, the most essential element of the universe is a paradox that moves and stays still. And you must learn, like light, to move between places, between memory and present, stories and truth. In this way, you can hear the story of light.

Promises

The reason we went to England the first summer, the summer I was ten, lay in a long-ago promise. And a long-ago philosopher named Heracleitus.

As my father told it, Heracleitus believed that the world was always in flux. Everything I knew—the grass and trees, the sky arching overhead, even my own mother and father—was always changing. This was the principle of things that stayed put and things that moved, the stone and the river, home and travel. And out of the strife of opposites, like fire and water, would come a perfect, eternal harmony.

The night my father left his village in British Guiana for the United States, my grandmother stood at the top of the verandah stairs, weeping as she tried to sweep him back inside with her long black hair. But my father was very clever. He stepped to the other side of the water trench and called to his favorite sister, Inez. "You take care of our mother, and I'll take care of all you sisters," he promised. "And Inez, I'll send you money so you can buy pretty dresses, win yourself a rich man who going to buy you anything you want."

But when my father got to New York, he forgot about his promise to Inez. Instead, he fell in love with my mother, a secretary named Sonia Markowitz. As a young woman, my mother was a beauty who bewitched men. She wore her hip-length hair in two braids coiled about her head in a lustrous, thick halo. My Jewish grandfather forbade my mother from marrying the strange foreigner with his crazy meshuga-talk. Lovelorn, my father used to stand underneath my mother's Brooklyn apartment in hopes of catching a glimpse of her shaking out her splendid hair.

One night she appeared at her window. Spilling from her hands was a blanket that she flung toward him, and covered his face and hands. My father realized the blanket was made of the bristly strands of her hair. "If you'll marry me like this," she said, and thrust her shorn head into the night air, "I will run away with you."

Back in their village, when Inez read the letter from her brother Warren that announced his marriage, she was furious. What about *her* dresses and *her* bangles, her rich man? She remembered the night my father had left, how his promise had burned a hunger in her. She'd imagined the swoosh of her bell-shaped skirt as her brother lifted her over the roof, into the sky and overseas to another man, whose hands brimmed with gifts of gold and silk.

In a spiteful heat, she tore up the letter, packed her belongings, and ran away to Georgetown. There she boarded a boat bound for England, with two hundred pounds and a secretarial school certificate folded into her pocketbook.

The night before Inez's boat was to land in Dover, a man stood next to her on the deck and put his hand on the small of her back. Inez was impressed—she'd spent her whole life among boys who shyly stepped by the water trench when she passed, or others who pulled her into the bottomhouse, their mouths dark flowers opening with need.

This man seemed so city-like, dressed in a tailored suit, fedora cocked low over his eyes. His name was Vijay and he was off to England, like her, to find a better life. She offered him a dried hibiscus flower from her hat. He invited her to go down to his berth to get warm. "Folks like us, we got to take care of each other," he told her, stroking her cheek. "We like brother and sister."

Lying on his skinny bunk, she remembered her own brother as he waved to her from the gate, black hair gleaming, so like her own wavy hair now spread in Vijay's fingers. While Vijay made love to her, Inez felt the jade-green sea leak beneath her fingernails. Her flesh was melting into water itself. She loved this slip-sliding, Vijay moving above. First one Inez, who covered her nipples with country shyness; then another, who hooked her foot around a strange man's thigh. When she woke the next morning in her own cabin, she found one hundred pounds missing from her purse.

Inez rushed onto the deck, where she spotted Vijay strolling toward the gangplank chatting with a pretty English girl. The other passengers watched in astonishment as Inez hurled herself into the air, then pulled him down until they both tumbled off the boat and the water slapped them cold. Inez didn't know how to swim, but she did know how to make her body strong with anger. They fished her out of the water, and Inez could not stop laughing at the thought of Vijay's bobbing fedora, his frightened eyes at the sight of the mad sea woman who chased him down and snatched back her floating pound notes.

In London, Inez gathered her hurt into her pocketbook, made the rounds of employment agencies, and found a job in a firm that sold china statues of apple-cheeked milkmaids and dour farmers. Her boss was Tom Lacey, a ginger-haired man who left small gifts, such as Belgian chocolate and aerograms for writing to her family, on her desk blotter. During their lunch hour, she and Tom took walks in Hyde Park, where he bored her with his talk about the communist party, of which he was a loyal member. One evening Tom walked her to her boarding-house door, pressed his lips to hers, and asked her to marry him. All she could think was: How dry his lips.

The next Saturday, Inez boarded a train to Brighton, where she sat down, stripped off her wool stockings, and plunged her feet into the cold pebbles. She did not love Tom Lacey. His white skin puckered in knots around his knuckles. He was a penny-pincher, and his droning on about the evils of capitalism annoyed her. Inez sat for hours, waiting for some sign to scrawl above the chalky cliffs and tell her what to do. She remembered

Vijay leaning over her, how his neck swayed in rhythm with the boat. She'd hoped it could remain that way forever, a wet slippery rocking, no solid stops.

A woman in a plaid coat unfolded a deck chair and set down a picnic basket a few feet from her. The woman's thermos rolled across the pebbles, and she called out, "There's a dear, will you pick that up for me?" When Inez handed back the thermos, the woman remarked, "I saw you there before, sitting by yourself."

Inez's mood lifted. A friend, she thought. "I don't know many people here," she replied.

"Where you from, dear?"

"British Guiana."

The woman unscrewed her thermos and took a sip. She did not offer any of her drink to Inez. "You alone, then?"

Inez nodded. The woman sipped, and steam curled from her cup. Inez took a breath, then explained, "I didn't know a soul when I arrived, not anybody. I met this man, Tom, he hired me at first——" She trailed off, embarrassed. A line of concern creased the woman's forehead. She didn't seem to be following.

"You looking for a job, then? Because the Wedgeworth Inn is needing girls. And they've been so pleased with the ones they've found. You seem clean and quiet."

At that moment, the words fell right out of Inez. She looked at her dark legs, cut off at the ankles, surrounded by smooth, pale stones. When she turned to gaze at the ocean's horizon, a wave of pent-up memories struck her, hard. She felt the sea enter her, carrying bits of her old life: her brothers bicycling off to school each morning in their starched white shirts; she and her sisters, left behind, crouched in the dark bottomhouse as they peeled mangoes. She remembered her mother weeping at the top of the stairs the night her brother fled. She could not stay solid, could not stop the flood of tears that poured down her cheeks.

She jumped up and lunged toward the sea, thinking for a wild moment that she could swim back to Guiana. Then she halted. It was too late, she realized. Her brother had forgotten her. She was trapped on this dry little island with these dry, pale people. And while Tom Lacey left the air still around her heart, only he could protect her from horrid women with thermoses, give her peace and harmony of the soul.

Though her mind was made up, Inez wept for weeks, all through the wedding preparations. Right away Tom bought a house and took care of everything, the Hoovering and the Saturday shopping and the gardening. Inez cried every night. Tom began to get mad. All this crying and the house would rot. He started his nightly fires, for in fire Tom saw a great redemption; he believed that a dry soul was a wise soul.

In a corner of the garden, he burned the wrappers from chocolates Inez bought when she was homesick and blue, and the frayed slippers she shuffled around in, the ones she'd purchased with her first paycheck. Tom meant to do away with too much longing for all that she couldn't have. Fire, he knew, reduced everything to ash.

Inez began to change. As she watched the fires glow in the garden each night, her skin went tight with heat. Her heart wrung itself out. Her bad dreams dried up. She even started to like England. She took to cutting her hair in a curly cap and hushing the sunny vowels of her accent.

This was the new Inez, marching down Greenford Avenue in her sensible cork-soled shoes, a jittery smile fixed to her face.

England was manners, and manners often meant hoarding one's feelings like a bushel of onions. Her lips cracked from too many thank yous.

Still, she kept some of her old village ways. When Tom told her of his raise, she smiled and said, "That's good, dear. They gone and blow good wind on you." When her neighbor Mrs. Gregory wore a crimson dress with a daffodil-bright cardigan, Inez told her, "Oh no, dear. Yellow and red are bad together. That's blood and birth, and you don't want to be mixing the two."

One night Inez woke in a panic, flew down the stairs, and attacked the larder, pulling down rice and potatoes and biscuits. Throat parched, she wanted more: the sun's melon ripeness drenching her village road, the sea leaking beneath her fingernails.

"Inez!" Tom called from the stairs. "Inez, what are you doing awake at this hour?"

In a dank corner of the larder, her fingers fumbled upon a net bag, bumpy with fruit. She drew a plum to her mouth, broke its skin, teeth aching as she sucked the cold, shredded heart of flesh. Doused in sweet fruit, she was flooded with thoughts of the lush cotton dresses she'd hoped for, cool gold bangles on her wrists, everything her brother had promised. Her body shook with longing and rage. Then her hands fell upon the old aerograms, hidden in a coffee can. Quickly she pulled out a sheet and wrote to my mother, fast and furious.

Dear Sonia,

We have never met, though I feel as if you have been whispering outside my kitchen window for many years now. I have decided to shout back. How is my brother doing? How old is my niece now? Why don't you come and stay the summer with us?

Love to all,

I.

P.S. If you do come, don't forget your rubber boots.

P.P.S. Do you think you might bring a set of percale double sheets? They're so dear over here. And if you happen to find an oval tablecloth, Tom prefers green. Much appreciated.

P.P.P.S. One more thing! I hear they have lovely drip-dry blouses in America. Think you might squeeze a couple in? Tom adores blue on me and would be ever so grateful.

And some panty hose would do me good. Cream or coffee shade would be fine, dear. Tom so loves when my legs are done up nice.

After Inez was done writing, she grew calm. Her mind was clear. Because she knew. The hunger her brother had torn open in her would be filled. He would return to her, making good on his promise, hands brimming with beautiful gifts.

I was never sure if I should believe the story of my mother's cutting off her hair to run away with my father, or whether my aunt really jumped into the sea. After all, my mother hardly bewitched my father anymore. My parents often fought, and divided the world according to their desires. My mother used words like "romance," "getaways," "Valentine's Day." My father was baffled. He had no idea what she meant. "Here," he'd say, and pull his American Express card out of his wallet, "buy yourself a new coat, a nice dress." With a grunt, he'd go into his study to grade papers and leave my mother to wander around the house, dressed in her pretty outfits, a girl waiting for a signal from afar.

That was why, the instant she received my aunt's letter, she declared we should go to England for the summer. My father agreed, though he decided to stay behind to teach summer school; he would join us in one month's time. At the airport, when I cried because my father wasn't coming with us on the plane, he told me, "Don't be afraid, my little one. Just remember. Ours is a restless family, flicking between continents, swimming in new elements. Now you can travel between two places and still be yourself. Just like light. How lucky you are."

To me, England was a perfect picture of balance and order. Everything composed itself into small, manageable parts: the red-roofed houses set down in neat rows, the little cars that blinked their headlights as they eased to a stop at the zebra walk. There was my uncle's prim garden, with its gay bunches of rose-bushes, pink petals sprinkled on the ground, as if my aunt had reached out the bedroom window and flung torn tissues from her vanity table.

I also had my cousin George, who was like a twin to me. He was eleven, one year older than I, with the same shock of straight black hair and black eyes. His skin was darker, though, a ma-hogany brown. The first week in England, I made my mother buy me sandals with the punched-hole design, just like George's, and trimmed my hair short in a Beatles cut, same as his. My little cousin Timmy had just turned five, and didn't look anything like George and me, with his small eyes and yellow skin.

My uncle Tom gave me a new idea of a father, as someone who always fretted about small matters, such as whether the rubbish was taken out, whether George ate his potatoes, or whether the garden was properly weeded. He was a pain, yet I liked it too. Here in England, everything was not filled with strife and conflict but was perfect, orderly, and sane.

Except for one thing—my father's promise to Inez, which my mother had not forgotten.

Once we'd settled in Sudbury, she blazed through the house, clicking down the halls in her high heels and noting the many things that were wrong—the broken tank chain in the separate lavatory, the kitchen with no refrigerator, just a larder, with its fold-back door. Worst of all, she said, Uncle Tom and Aunt Inez had no telephone!

At the end of our second week, after drawing up a list of what she wanted my father to bring to England, my mother marched to the corner and called him collect from a pillar box.

"About that telephone," she remarked to my aunt and uncle at tea later. "What if there's an emergency? What will you do then?"

"Run down to the pub and take a pint at the same time," my uncle replied, winking. Uncle Tom was proud, stiff, and he didn't like anything showy. Nice things he sniffed at. He scraped the bottom of his teacup on its saucer, so it made a wet, rubbing sound. "We've got along fine so far, mind you."

"You hear what Sonia was saying the other day, Tom?" Aunt Inez chirped. "They've got a car over there in New York. And a stereo too."

"They've got crime and expensive health care as well," Uncle Tom answered.

"Imagine," Aunt Inez said with a sigh. "I remember when my sister Didi and I used to wash Warren's one good shirt for school. That poor boy had nothing, not even the books to read for his exams. Now he's an important professor in America, buying all that!"

My aunt spoke with a funny, lilting accent—half Caribbean, half British—always pecking at what should or shouldn't be. Her eyes, dark with envy, kept flashing to my mother's Italian pumps. I wished I could tell her the real story behind those shoes: how my father had bought them for my mother after she'd locked herself for a whole day in her bedroom, sobbing that my father didn't love her anymore. My father always bought my mother expensive things after a particularly bad fight.

"Dad," George chimed in. "When do we get to go to America? Everybody there seems so rich."

"Don't be stupid," Tom said. "A few Rockefellers is all. Everyone else is bad off. And don't let your uncle Warren's success story fool you otherwise."

"But Sonia says that's not true," Aunt Inez protested. "The professors at Warren's college make a good salary. And Warren got a promotion last year with a nice raise—"

My uncle jumped up, teacup and saucer crashing to the table. "Enough of this money talk!" His eyes blazed at me and George. "George, let's show your American cousin how to make a decent fire."

I nervously followed them out to the garden. George disappeared into the shed and returned with a stack of newspapers, which he dumped near a clearing in a corner where two hedges met. My uncle kneeled on the grass and arranged the wood scraps into a pyramid. "Don't just stand like that, George," he said, "there's more in the back."

We each lugged out things my uncle had cleared from the house in anticipation of our stay. There was more piled in the shed, bound bundles of newspaper, flattened cardboard boxes, Timmy's soiled blankets and the broken rods of his old crib. My arms began to ache, but Uncle Tom huffed and barked orders like the thickheaded Klink on *Hogan's Heroes*. "Hurry up!" he shouted, face flushed. "That's it, Meggie! A good fire means not leaving a bit of rubbish behind!"

I struggled to run, my uncle's voice egging me on. "That's right!" he cheered, and rubbed his palms together. "This is going to be a splendid fire! Splendid!" George's elbow cut my side as he shoved me away and struggled with a thick bundle of towels and clothes tied with twine. Eyes smarting, I pushed against his back and streaked ahead, then dumped my uncle's old accounting ledgers with a proud clatter.

"Dad," my cousin cried as the pile slipped, dropping to the grass. "I can't carry any more! My arms hurt and my shoes are pinching my toes. They're too small!"

"You finish what you've started," my uncle told him. "Never leave a job undone."

Uncle Tom bent down and heaved the bundle toward us. It wobbled for a moment, a fat white ball, and spun toward my face. Out of the corner of my eye, I saw George limp forward, but I elbowed past him and thrust my arms out. A moment later the bundle slammed into my face. A rush of air was sucked from my ribs. Rough twine cut my lip, but I still clutched the heavy mound.

"Excellent job!" My uncle strode up to me. "I can see you've got your father's ambition too, Meggie." He brushed my throbbing mouth. When he pulled his hand away, I saw that a droplet of my blood glistened on his finger.

In a quavery voice I asked, "Is that bad?"

"Not at all. One must simply be careful with ambition, Megan. Without a proper sense of balance, it can eat you up."

Then my uncle yelled to George, who kneeled by the fire scrunching handfuls of newspaper into the pile. "All right, let's get started."

He drew a box of matches from his pocket, scraped a match until it caught, and jabbed at the fire with a piece of lit kindling. Thin flames licked at the balled-up newspaper.

"Are you mad at my mom?" I asked him.

He threw twigs into the fire and answered in a low voice, "The way I see it, Meggie, to want too much is a bad hunger that will take you to bad places. People like Inez and your father, they come over from their poor countries and they want too much. Your mother encourages this, and that's wrong. Inez and your father, they think about their sisters and brother in that old house and they get upset. They have no self-control. They are cursed with the hunger of the past."

He wagged a pair of garden shears in the air. "Now George, let's see about those shoes of yours." He poked the edges of George's sandals. Flames leaped higher from the rubbish pile. George began to whimper. "Curl your toes, young man!"

"Dad!"

"Do as I say!"

George looked sick, his cheeks puffed out. I shut my eyes tight. I could hear the faint rasp of metal on leather. "Dad!"

George shrieked. My eyes flew open, for I expected blood to spurt from my cousin's feet. Then I saw his white-socked toes peek out like eggs in a cup.

"Never waste!" my uncle said, as he tossed the leather crescents into the flames.

Afternoons, George and I took the few shillings and pence my mother and aunt gave us, then ran down the block to the toy shop to buy plastic GI soldiers, and paper kites that lifted into the air like giant flowers, splitting down the center when the wind blew too hard. We staked out a hiding place in the garden shed, where it smelled damp, of peat moss and splintery rotted wood.

Usually George and I tried to get rid of Timmy, through mean and elaborate ruses. "There's a troll waiting for you in the furniture," we would tell him. By the time he had scrambled on hands and knees under the parlor table, we would have run through the gate and across the street. The moment we reached the woods, our minds brimmed with fanciful games.

At the top of Horsendon Hill sat a large concrete block that we called the bench. The front was cut into a deep, L-shaped step, which made a surprisingly comfortable seat. Its true purpose remained a mystery. Uncle Tom told me it had once been the base for a statue of a local lord. George and I relished dozens of interpretations of what it might be—a marker for a secret tunnel, pillar of a mansion long since burned, trap door for a special television studio where my newly discovered show *The Avengers* was filmed.

The morning after the fire I woke sore inside. The cut on my lip smarted. I put on my favorite shorts and polo shirt and went into the garden, where I kneeled before the circle of singed grass left by Uncle Tom's fire. Gently I lifted a burnt leaf, fragile as a sand dollar, and squeezed. Wispy flakes sifted in my palm. Something was crumbling inside me too, but I didn't know what. I only knew I didn't have a good feeling about my father's arrival the next week.

"Come on," George said, and nudged me in the ribs. "I'll race you to the woods."

We tore through the gate and paused at the curb. Greenford Avenue widened with promise. Then we ran toward Horsendon Woods, charging past the vaulting trees. I did not understand what had come over me. I was scared of something that lay beyond us, and my heart knocked in my ribs as we pounded up the slope and flopped down on the hill. Below was a sea of leaning grass; the fluted-roof houses faded like choppy waves in the distance.

George rolled over. "So what's your dad like, Meggie? He sounds super."

"He is," I agreed. "When he gets here, he'll take us on walks and tell us stories."

"What kind of stories?"

I thought about this. Which father would join us? The perfect one, who talked a private language with me, or the one who left my mother alone in their bedroom, surrounded by a crest of rumpled sheets? The father who told stories and promised so much, or the father who disappointed?

"Let's see," I said. "My dad, he's an old navy captain. He wears a patch on his eye. And the top of this hill is the garage for his ship."

"What's his ship look like, Meggie?"

"It's really a big brown Pontiac car," I told George excitedly, as one idea mounted into another. "It's got power steering and air-conditioning. In the back is the treasure he wants to bring back to win the heart of the queen. And you're a pirate who wants to steal everything."

George shook his head in confusion. "What's the treasure, Meggie?"

Remembering my mother's call to my father from the pillar box, I exclaimed, "Lots! There's a stereo and Hot Wheels model cars and an Instamatic camera and a banana-seat bicycle——"

George's eyes brightened. "We're going to have all that?"

A sweet sensation washed over me. I yanked on his sleeve and started running down the hill. George jumped to his feet and flapped his arms like wings. "Hey ho!" he shouted. His voice drifted in the breeze. "We're going to have a stereo!"

He flew into the air and tumbled after me, knocked me breathless to the ground. Laughing, we raced to the top of the hill and rolled down, again and again, until we made ourselves sick. Later, as we lay in the flattened weeds, waiting for the sky to stop its giddy spin, I suddenly knew I couldn't live without George. I loved him so much that when I thought of him gone from me, I saw a hole between my arms, where the wind could blow.

When we got up and strolled home for teatime, as if reading my thoughts, George put a soft hand on my arm and said, "Poor Meggie. Who are you going to marry when you grow up? Me or your dad?"

The evening before my father's arrival, my aunt and mother lugged full laundry baskets into the garden. While they pinned towels to the line, I hid in the narrow alley between the shed and house. Twilight fell around us, the sky like a glass bowl emptying blue powder.

"I'm worried about Tom," my aunt remarked. "We have to be careful about those things you want to get for us. I don't want to set him off again."

"The problem is, I've already spoken to Warren," my mother said. "And if there's one thing he knows how to do, it's spend money." She sighed. "I only wish I could get him to notice me."

"Don't be silly! My brother is always in his own world with his big ideas. And look at all he's given you. I'd take one of your pretty dresses any day!"

"I want more than that, Inez. A man isn't a paycheck." My mother's voice was soft and bleating; she sounded like a child crying for milk.

I bore down hard on my heels, wishing I could jam myself into a small rock. I hated when my mother talked this way.

"That's my point. Warren got a different way of showing what he feels. And you can't go making a big fuss all the time. You got to move quiet and you get what you want."

Just then, I stumbled out from behind the shed, rubbing my sore kneecaps. My mother and my aunt turned their heads. "Megan!" my mother cried. "What are you doing there, spying on us!"

"This child." Gently my aunt tapped my ears. "In Guyana they say a child who listens to old people's secrets is like a fish that fills its gills with too much water and can't hold up its head."

"My head's not too heavy," I objected.

"Maybe not now." She smiled. "You wait."

Aunt Inez lifted the basket and disappeared through the

kitchen door. Although she had scolded me, I didn't mind. I knew that behind her fussiness lay the old Inez, the one I'd heard about in a story, who lay inside a boat with the sea sliding inside her skin. As the twilight deepened, I imagined the garden turning into a great blue-green pond. I saw my father swim through the gate, toward us, and my cousin dive from his bedroom window, splashing toward him.

My mother's arms glowed, white and beautiful, as she called softly to me. I ran into her embrace, and the air streamed cool at my sides. We stood together to watch the stars that sparkled above. My mother wore a blue-striped dress with a matching belt that made her waist look small and feminine.

"Maybe I should listen to Inez," she reflected. "Your father must care, since he agreed to this trip. And it's so good here. The charming pillar boxes and the lovely gardens! Next week Uncle Tom is going to take us sightseeing in the city. Would you like that?"

"Can George come?"

"Of course. We're a family now. We do everything together. When your father is here, we'll go to the National Gallery and shop on Regent Street." She took a deep breath. "It will be so wonderful, just like when I first married your father—"

I pressed myself against my mother and felt the soft tremble of her heart. Drawing back, I said, "I have a surprise for you."

Her jaw tightened into a smile. "Oh, my sweet grown-up Meggie. What surprise do you have for your silly mother?"

"Let me show you." I led her by the hand into the house and upstairs.

After I shut the bedroom door, I pulled her hair from its pins and spread it across her shoulders. I dragged my fingers through the strands, amazed at the sparks that jumped from the silky blackness. Then I told her to undress. While she sat naked on the bed, her lovely breasts balanced on her slender torso, I helped her put on mauve stockings that fit snug on her firm thighs; a red tailored suit with a jacket that flared at her hips; an abalone comb that shone behind one ear.

"If you wear this tomorrow, my daddy won't be able to stop looking at you," I told her as I rubbed cocoa butter into her palms.

She blushed. "What a wise lady you are! What else can you tell me?"

"He'll take you in his arms and carry you away to sightsee on a double-decker bus."

"Anything more, my little prophet?"

I halted. I did not believe a word I had just said. Yet I knew my mother lived for the hope that one day my father would again turn his gaze to her, as he had when she was a young woman by her bedroom window. I took her again into my arms, and prayed, Please, please, Daddy, love her better than you do me.

By late morning the sun was a gold medallion on a sky of painted blue silk. George and I sat on the front steps, dressed identically in navy shorts, maroon pullovers, and crisp permanent-press shirts. My uncle was stooped over the rose-bushes, clipping at dead leaves.

Soon a long black taxicab pulled up to the curb. A tall man emerged from the rear door and wiped aside a curl of hair that had fallen over his brow. My father was much bigger than I remembered; he filled the gate opening and blocked out Uncle Tom.

He came up the path with loud, heavy steps, chin raised, eyes fixed on the top of the door. His suitcases bumped against his legs. I remained sitting, knees pressed together, hoping he would first notice my mother. She stood poised in the doorway. In her new flared jacket, she resembled an origami bird, stiff and angular.

"Hello, Warren," she said.

His face softened with warmth. "Look at Meggie! How much you've grown! Come, darling, give your old man a hug!"

A sharp ache cut through me when I saw my mother stumble backward into a triangle of darkness, hand covering her mouth. Then my father seemed to remember himself and stepped forward to kiss her cheek.

My aunt waited behind my mother, hands in her apron. She and my father warily eyed each other, until my aunt put her arms around his shoulders, briefly hugged him, and stepped back to pat the bottom curls of her hair. "Come now," she said. "Time for a little refreshment."

In the parlor, where tea and biscuits were laid out, my father and my aunt sat at opposite ends of the room. From the bookcase, Uncle Tom brought out the large flat box of chocolates, which he kept hidden behind a ceramic vase. George crept over to the table where Uncle Tom had put the box. "Ah, ah!" Uncle Tom scolded, and slapped him on the wrist. "Mind your manners, young man, and offer some to the others first." Obediently

George offered the box to each person, then put a few into his mouth.

My father was busy gazing around the parlor. I could see that the room must have seemed shabby to him, with its diamond-print walls faded and the tile fireplace leaky with drafts. "Now listen, Tom, Sonia called me," he said in his booming voice. "I'd like to buy you a few things. A refrigerator. Maybe a stereo."

My uncle sat up straight and rubbed the bottom of his tumbler across his knee, back and forth. "That's quite all right," he said. "No need."

My mother looked as if she wanted to disappear into the sofa. "Warren, please," she whispered. "Not now."

"Come on!" My father inched forward in his chair, and his voice grew high and excited, exploding into the same lilt as my aunt's. "I want to do it, Tom! This here my sister, man! Why she have to carry those groceries every day! Why you think I work the whole year long, if I can't spend my money on my own family?"

Aunt Inez angrily pushed her feet into her slippers. "No more talk about this," she said, embarrassed.

"I remember back in Lettur Kenny village!" my father went on. "You and Didi have to walk a whole mile to the market. Why I can't buy my sister a refrigerator?"

"Because that was before, Warren," Uncle Tom said firmly. "This is now." He stood and banged out of the room.

That night I curled up on George's bed while my parents quarreled in his room. My father's suitcase was opened on the eiderdown, and my mother had her back to me as she slammed shoes into the floor of the wardrobe. Not so loud, my father complained. He had changed into an undershirt and a pair of old tan pants that drooped off his hips, so he didn't seem nearly as big as before.

"Don't you see?" My mother wagged a brown loafer by its heel. "You can't buy yourself back into the family, Warren. You have to *be* here first."

He dropped down on the bed. "You yourself told me the woman drag home those groceries every day and this man so cheap he won't buy her a refrigerator!"

"Shhh." My mother crossed the room and loudly deposited the shoe in the wardrobe. She pushed clothes around and rattled hangers on their rod, as if trying to drown out my father's tactlessness. "Tom is very proud, Warren."

"Uncle Tom says, 'No waste!' " I threw in.

"Hush, Megan. This is between adults."

My father didn't hear either of us. He was busy peeling off his socks. "Listen here, Sonia! I'm not a boy in a village anymore! I'm a professor now! I brought my American dollars!" From his pockets, he brought out fistfuls of bills. The furrow in his brow was momentarily relaxed. "You laugh! You think I'm a fool? I know I shocked the man!"

Inside the narrow cave of the wardrobe, my mother's laughs echoed. "Oh, no," she said. "There you go again." She stepped out, her hair full around her shoulders. Like my father, without her dress clothes, she seemed different, less angular. I noticed the soft, freckled slope of her shoulders as she went to my father and stroked his hair. He grabbed her around the waist and shook his fist in her face. "You know what this is?"

He flung the bills into the air. "This is all mine!" I watched him spin in the center of the room, tossing out clumps of dollars.

His laughter climbed higher and higher as more bills dropped around us, a swirl of wrinkled green leaves.

Ever since that day the peaceful balance in our Sudbury home was tipped. My father entered our lives like an extra book squeezed onto an already full shelf. There were no plans to go to the city to sightsee or to visit the National Gallery. Instead, there were books on the pre-Socratics and several sets of colored note-cards that my father had brought in his second suitcase.

Afternoons, when I tired of playing with George, I helped my father. Each notecard color—yellow, cream, blue, green—corresponded to a different element—fire, air, water, earth—and we divided up George's bedroom with small piles on the floor. Then my father wrote down his thoughts on the cards and gave them to my mother to type. As a special touch, she tied the typescript pages with a violet sash. At moments like this, I loved my family, loved its wholeness, though the balance never held.

Nights, my father and I resumed our talks. George was jealous, but this was too delicious: leaving the house, my fingers laced in my father's, as we walked Horsendon Hill to sit for hours on the bench. "Why you have to push that girl so much?" my aunt would say when we returned, before hustling me upstairs and tucking me into bed with a hot-water bottle. But my aunt's ministrations were a waste. I wanted to go on those walks. They made me feel chosen for an unexplained role.

"Daddy," I asked one night, touching the pocked surface of the bench. "What do you think this is?"

"It's a bench."

"What was it before?" I persisted.

"There is no before. It's a bench because I'm sitting on it."

"Maybe it was meant for something else. It doesn't really look like a bench."

"That doesn't matter, Meggie. A thing is what we use it for. Not what it was built to be."

I chewed over this one. "But the other day George and I pretended that it was empty and there were guns inside. Couldn't it be a secret hiding place?"

"It could," he answered smoothly. "But that's not how we think in philosophy. Take, for instance, a tree. First it's a tree, then it's cut, and now it's a log. Then the log is cut so it's a board. Next it's sanded and nailed to other boards and it's a table. Then—"

"Somebody chops it up and turns it into firewood."

"Exactly." He smiled at me. "You see, Meggie, when we name something, we're really just describing what it means to us."

"Why can't it just be a tree?"

"What about its seed?"

I was stumped. Telescoping in my mind was an endless succession of origins—the seed born from a drop in a pod, the drop a cluster of fibers and hairs, the hairs a glob of invisible cells. One question tunneled into more questions, exhausting me. I wanted something different. I wanted this hard, gritty block of concrete to burst alive as something else, the way it did when George and I played our games. Was that possible in my father's way of dividing up the world?

"Now, Meggie, this isn't just about trees. The same can be said about money. In America we pay in dollars. In England we use pounds. We're just giving it a name according to how we see it. Does that mean we know what money really is?"

"I guess not," I answered, a little confused.

"That's the same problem with light. We don't know what it is. A photon is actually a relationship between us and something out there. It can't be described because"—his hand made a sweeping gesture toward the dark sky—"the universe is unpredictable."

As we started down Horsendon Hill, hand in hand, I let this word roll under my tongue and savored its dusky, mysterious taste. *Unpredictable.* The trees parted, revealed shadows in the distance. Now these woods might be so much more. I could see further, into the secrets that sometimes flashed behind my family's faces. As we reached the street, I was sure my father had taught me an important lesson.

After that, I began to watch our family carefully. The more I looked, the more I saw pockets of puzzling behavior. Every morning my mother woke me with one brisk, angry shake, and just as briskly left the room to run water in a teapot downstairs. Uncle Tom grew more withdrawn. He neglected his precious roses, so they hung on their stems with heavy, raggedy heads; he let the rubbish overflow in the shed.

I also noticed differences between George and me. Once, when he stole chocolates from the hiding place, Uncle Tom hit him with the back of a hairbrush. I envied my cousin. He was punished and everything was over the next day. If I did something wrong, it seemed to linger, like a bad odor, or something my parents would use to prod each other. They never worried about my moral fiber; this gave me a peculiar feeling of helplessness.

And while George held most grown-ups in awe, I thought of them as just like the universe my father described—outrageous and unpredictable—particularly when it came to money. When no one was looking, my mother bought an extra two pounds of meat at the butcher's, even though Uncle Tom had forbidden her to contribute to the household shopping.

He was especially incensed when my father began to give George and me money. Every night my father emptied his pockets and put the change on the dressertop. At the end of the week he divided the coins into two neat piles, then dropped each into George's and my waiting hands.

"Young man," he explained to my cousin the first time, "I've always said that knowledge in the hands of the wrong person is a waste. Since I don't understand the money system here, I'm leaving it to you to spend these properly."

"Listen up, I've done some reading too, Warren," Uncle Tom said when he learned of my father's gift to my cousin and me. "I've looked at your books, and one of them says, 'It isn't good for men to get all they wish to get.' "

"True," my father replied. "But the problem with some of those Greek fellows is, they were kind of stingy. And when it comes to my family, they must never be wanting. To be poor is to always be hungry, even in the mind."

One Saturday morning, as I was spooning porridge from my bowl, I looked up to see my mother push through the rear parlor door, a slant of misery across her face. She was still in her robe, belt jammed into a knot. Without a word, she went to the sink and began rattling pots.

"What's the matter?" I asked.

She didn't turn around. "Nothing."

My mother's and aunt's whispers became a furious hiss by the sink. My stomach sank. I hated days like these. They reminded me of when my parents fought at home, and the house felt large and empty, the three of us bumping around the rooms like eggs loose in a carton. "You know the way he is," I heard my mother say. "He says he doesn't have time to go into the city." My aunt put a hand around her shoulders and they rocked for a moment, hips touching. A few minutes later my mother slipped back upstairs.

I waited ten minutes before I followed her.

My parents' bedroom door was open a few inches. "Don't," I heard my father say.

"Warren, please."

Curious, I kneeled beside the slender opening. I could see my father, slumped on the mattress edge, dressed only in his trousers, his nipples like two bits of dark chocolate. The round of his stomach rose and sank. My mother stood between his knees. She now wore a silk kimono, splashed with a rain of orange petals. Elbows flashing, she drew her fingers through his hair. My father's breathing grew faster. His face was in her belly, her kimono parted until her breasts tumbled free. For a moment his hands cupped their soft bottoms, then dropped away.

"If you only knew," he said. "Sometimes I can't think straight. I can't do it—"

"Don't be silly."

"Everything I write, it's no good. I'm a failure, Sonia."

Gently my mother pushed at his shoulder, until he eased back on the bed and his knees swung open. I knew I shouldn't stay, but I could not stop watching my parents fumble and move. My mother's head disappeared between his thighs and a moan escaped my father's throat. "Sonia, no——"

"Hush, darling. Just relax——"

Sunlight gathered around my father. He was larger than anything in the room. My mother shrank to thin bone. He grew wings of gold that covered them both in a rocking motion. My head ached. I wished they would take me with them. But no space was left for me. There was only my father, rising higher, while my mother dangled loose from his waist. They were lost to me. She tugged and they fell in a clumsy heap to the bed. Now they were just my ordinary mother and father, he snatching at his clothes.

"What is it now?" my mother cried.

His arms flopped helplessly on the bed. "I'm sorry, Sonia," he answered. "I can't. I just can't."

I crept to my room. Through the window I saw my cousin kick a soccer ball across the grass, but I didn't want to join him. The sight of my mother and father in their bedroom left a dark stain on my thoughts. They had mingled into me and I into them. I stayed inside until I heard my father's cheery voice down the corridor. For a moment I was confused. Then I remembered it was time for our Saturday handout.

Nothing showed on my father's face while he sorted his

money. My mother and my aunt had crowded around the dresser, and their eyes blazed with a strange, sheepish excitement.

"Hurry," my mother urged. "Tom could come back any minute now."

The coins made a satisfying clink as he poured them into my cousin's open palms. When I touched my own pile of silver and copper, a mischievous spark caught in my mind.

My aunt frowned. "How can you give George so much money when he's so dreamy!" she complained. "He'll lose it right away."

"Oh, no," I interjected, dropping my coins into my pocket. "We're going to spend them on an underwater diver. Isn't that right, George?" I nudged my cousin in the ribs. He gave me a meek nod.

My aunt didn't object too loudly, since my father put a twenty-pound note into her palm. I smiled as I remembered my aunt's story, for she was getting what she wanted from my father. He led us downstairs to the kitchen, where my aunt and my mother whispered and pointed to the sink, and agreed to meet at a Wembley restaurant later.

I liked the air of secrecy and promise that stirred through the rooms. It made everything seem more hopeful and abundant. After my mother, Aunt Inez, and Timmy left for Wembley, George and I raced down the block to the toy shop and bought our underwater diver. Then we returned home and locked ourselves in the bathroom and ran water in the tub.

"Not so much," George pleaded. "We're only supposed to fill it six inches."

"This is different," I told him, poking at the cellophane

package. "It's a *deep*-water diver." I lowered the diver and watched it unspool like a spider from its plastic strand, legs slowly pumping as it moved across the tub's bottom. "Maybe we can buy a boat too," I suggested. "So the diver can jump."

George gave me a dubious look. "We haven't any money left, Meggie. And they're awfully dear."

I clambered onto the tub's slippery edge and peered through the curtains to the garden below. My father was asleep in a deck chair, head lolled backward. This annoyed me. I wanted my father to be awake, so I might pry some more coins from him.

After I climbed down from my perch, George trailing behind, I went to the bedroom to check if there was any money left on the dresser. There wasn't, so we ran downstairs to where my father slept. He did not wake when we slammed out the kitchen door. His mouth hung open, and a slow grinding scraped out of his throat.

"Why don't we come back later?"

"It's right here." I pointed to the small bulge in his shirt pocket.

"Oh, no. My father'll take the belt to me." George backed away a few feet.

I reached a hand to my father's pocket and pulled out the folded bills. I could feel the warmth of his skin under his shirt. He never stirred.

"Put it back!" George cried. "It's just the coins he gives us."

The faded notes came unruffled in my palm. I reflected a moment, my thoughts speeding faster. "A coin is just a coin because we call it that," I reasoned. "And the coins add up to the same thing, like the money my dad wants to give us, so there's really no difference, right?"

George looked as though he might burst into tears. When he was flustered, his face was like a small brown parasol, shutting discreetly on itself. I charged down the path and through the gate, George wailing behind, "You can't take them all! You've got to give some back!"

George's whining made me want to buy as much and spend as outrageously as I could. At the toy shop, he watched with surprise while I pulled from the shelves not just one boat but two—a battery-operated racing model and a large yellow tugboat with snap-off dinghies. There was a hole in me that I needed to fill. With the two shillings left over, I purchased a bar of chocolate. Back home, we sprawled on the garden grass, played with our new boats and feasted on chocolate. My father was gone from his chair.

"My dad isn't going to like this." George pointed to the wrapping paper and plastic strewn around us. "We better put this away before someone sees." He took the chocolate bar from my hands, broke off a large piece, and popped it into his mouth.

"I have a better idea," I said. "He won't know if we get rid of the paper, right? Why don't we make a fire, like him?"

George started to protest, but I was already running across the garden, taken with my new idea. When I opened the shed door, I was hit with a funky odor. My stomach lurched. Around me loomed moldy piles, the rubbish Uncle Tom had let pile up in the past couple of weeks.

After finding the matchbox on the wooden shelf, I hugged a crisp stack of newspapers and joined George, who was already tossing the cardboard and plastic wrappers from our boats onto the rubbish heap. I tried to start the fire the way I'd seen Uncle Tom do, carefully building a triangle of dry kindling. Flame buds jumped in the oily creases of newspaper, then sank. I dropped match after match until flames were snaking between the wooden sticks.

When I kicked at the dirt, the tugboat rolled into the fire heap. Fascinated, I watched its tip soften to a dripping spout. I picked up a twig and poked dimples in its melting sides. One rubber dinghy cracked off its latches. A sour odor sifted into the air. I sneezed. The boat puffed into a fat golden ball on the newspaper. Any minute it might explode like a cartoon sun.

"This isn't good, Meggie," George whimpered. "Those boats are brand-new."

"Who cares? It's neat."

He tugged on my shirt. "Please, stop!"

"Shut up. Don't be such a chicken. We can always buy another one."

As my cousin begged me to stop, the more I wanted to steal money to buy brand-new toys, so the fire could climb higher, until we were surrounded by a delicious crackle of things burning and the promise of more to come. My eyelids itched. Smoke corkscrewed through the hedges.

"Meggie, stop it right now!" George's lips were a quivering weak line.

"I'll do what I want!" I screamed, and struck him, hard, across his face. His cheek softened like putty under my knuckles. This only made me want to hit him again. The troubles that had piled up since my father arrived—no visits to the city, my uncle's sullen moods, the strange sight of my mother at my father's waist—poured out. The fire mounted, and an ugly hunger roared in me, sprouted in my stomach and mouth and ears.

Someone gave a shout. George and I turned around, to see

two men making their way toward the house. One was my uncle, who walked determinedly through the gate, full string bags bouncing against his legs. Behind him a deliveryman in a blue uniform pushed a large cardboard box.

My uncle stopped short in front of the rosebushes and sniffed. "What's going on here?" he asked.

I swallowed, unable to say a word. George kicked at a tuft of grass. The shopping bags dropped to the ground; two oranges rolled in the grass. I suddenly noticed how thin my uncle's hair was on top, combed sideways to make up the difference.

"What are you two up to?" he demanded.

"Excuse me, sir," the deliveryman said. "This here One fifty-eight Greenford Avenue? Two ladies just came by, paid cash they did, and wanted this delivered."

"Not now," my uncle said, and hurried across the grass toward us. He slapped my cousin once across the cheek. George's head jerked backward. My eyes stung with tears. "It's me that did it!" I wanted to shout. I wished my uncle's hand would come thundering against my cheek, punish me in a sure way, scorch me clean.

Uncle Tom grabbed a long plank and swatted at the fire. Embers jumped over his head. Then I saw, squashed in the middle, like a garish centerpiece, our boats, now a lump of charred plastic. He tore up the path to the front door, the deliveryman calling behind, "Please, sir, it's just a signature!"

A moment later my uncle's voice rattled against the bathroom tiles. "Who filled the tub with water! George!" A door slammed. Voices spilled through the wall, my father's low rumble mingled with Uncle Tom's short, dry bursts.

"Promises!" Uncle Tom shouted. "You, coming here with all

your promises! This is *my* house! This is not the way I raised my son!"

"You!" my father yelled back. "You and your prideful ways! You know nothing! Every day I see my sisters with their shabby dresses and their no-good shoes! Every day I see my poor mother carry the water pot on her head like an old coolie woman. Now I come here, and you don't even have a decent iron so my sister can press your shirts!"

I listened to the thump and crash of objects on the floor, footsteps clomping down the stairs, then my father burst through the door. "Let's go," he said to me. The sharp tone in his voice told me I had no choice.

As we stepped through the gate, the deliveryman came forward and pushed the clipboard into my father's chest. My father paused, then a slow, triumphant smile swept across his face. It made me shiver, watching him sign his name with a cool, superior flourish. He grabbed me by the hand and led me down the street. I glanced back to the empty garden, where a thin trail of smoke drifted over the hedges.

Down the aisles of a fancy store my father sailed, past the display cases, shiny islands stacked high with merchandise. He'd stop, pick something out, pull his credit card from his wallet, and tap it on the glass counters. Since he rarely went shopping, he had no idea of prices. In the children's department, he bought me a pair of black patent-leather go-go boots that made a delicious *trra-ap* on the pavement, and an authentic plaid kilt that swung at my knees. Click! went the credit card. Click, click!

In another store he bought a crimson wool shawl for my mother, along with dozens of other presents for her and Aunt Inez and Uncle Tom and Timmy, which he let a saleswoman pick for him. I felt dizzy, too full. At the end, my father told me I could get something for George. I paused, not sure what to choose. First I picked out a set of miniature Scottish soldiers, and then I dragged him to the confectioner's, where we bought an enormous box of chocolates.

We went to the restaurant in Wembley and sat with our purchases around us, waiting. It was turning dark outside as my mother walked in, without my aunt. She looked wan, her eyes red-rimmed.

When she saw the packages, a perplexed look crossed her face. Her arms reached out, as if to brace against this vision. "Here, Sonia," my father said, cradling a perfume bottle in his hands. "Look what I have for you." My mother sank, stunned, into the booth. "And here." He waved a blue sweater like a flag.

My mother moaned softly as she bent over the new things. "What have you done?" she asked, and seized open a box. Tawny stockings unfurled to the seat. She grabbed the sweater from my father and clutched it to her chest. "This is madness!" she cried. I could tell she was pleased. My father and I exchanged relieved smiles. The dizzy feeling washed away. I knew it was worth seeing my mother so happy. She twisted around, a Scottish kilt pressed to her lap. "Madness!" she exclaimed once more.

I nearly lost my breath when my mother swooped to kiss my father on the mouth. It was the first time I had seen my parents kiss in public. For an instant I could imagine my mother when she threw her blanket of hair to my father, and let herself be carried away in his arms, into the night.

In the taxi home I sat in the back, packages next to me. The seats gave off a deep, cold odor and the reflections of the road lamps cascaded across the windshield, streamed along the sides. I watched the back of my mother's head, her brown hair caught and twirled in a tortoiseshell comb, as she chattered to my father. She was happier than I'd ever seen her, but it felt like a dangerous happiness. The car plunged deeper into the liquid evening, my mother's head bobbing, strands of hair on her cheek.

When we reached my aunt and uncle's, I ran inside the house, shouting for George. Before I knew it, I had reached the end of the corridor and entered the kitchen, where I immediately noticed a change. My aunt and uncle had a refrigerator! A small white one that fit exactly under the Formica counter, like a cardboard cake box. It looked as if it had always been there.

I went into the parlor, where my father was dropping armloads of packages on the floor. Aunt Inez, my mother, and Timmy were in a frenzy of ripping open presents, drowning in wrappers and crackling noise. Uncle Tom stood by the door, hands behind his back. Aunt Inez gasped and held up a pair of jade drop earrings. "They're too expensive!" she said, but unscrewed the plain gold posts from her lobes. A stream of boxes poured out—a celery-green cashmere V-neck pullover for Uncle Tom, a striped cap and mittens for Timmy, polo shirts and shorts for George, triangles of perfume for both Aunt Inez and my mother.

I kneeled beside George, who was setting his soldiers on the tile around the fireplace. He grinned when I pushed his box of chocolates toward him. "Tell me this," I said. "Is that refrigerator what the deliveryman brought today?"

He chewed a chocolate. His face was full of mystery. "I'd rather not say," he whispered. "It wouldn't be right."

My heart gave an angry turn, and I was about to reply, *"What* wouldn't be right? Why do you have to talk in secrets like that?" Then I stopped myself. Something had changed, a few hours before, when I stole the money from my father and started the fire. My cousin and I were being carried further apart, into separate currents that were there before we were born. George was drifting into a cove sheltered by Uncle Tom, while I was caught in the deep struggle between my parents.

The elements of my family joined, made their own predictable sense. My aunt stroked the gray-plumed collar of a new angora sweater. My mother paraded before the fireplace, a beauty queen, shawl pulled about her shoulders like a mane of burning hair. And there was my father, who gazed at us with a thin, cruel smile and saw only the truth of his own quest, and was blind to the others around him.

Then I realized Uncle Tom had left the room. I ran into the garden and found him by the hedges, where a strong fire was burning in the corner. He stood, erect and tall, feeding tissue wrap and shoe boxes to the climbing flames. Using one foot as an anchor, he tore the refrigerator box into thick brown slabs. He wrapped one in an oily rag and pushed it into the hot center of the fire. A *whoosh* swallowed the air. The tip was a glowing, red ball, which he used to poke the heap. Flames curled toward his hands. By now the fire was higher than any I'd seen; it reached the tops of the hedges.

"Uncle Tom," I asked, "why don't you come see the rest of the presents?"

He did not answer at first. "Go back inside," he finally said.

When I didn't move, he pushed my shoulder. "Leave me alone." I heard him say under his breath, "I read the book too. Fire is noble, water is ignoble."

His fingers fumbled with his buttons, and he stripped off his shirt and tossed it onto the flames. It billowed for an instant, a wide angry blue, and sank beneath a strip of wood. He bent down and carefully untied his shoes, and clapped the soles together before he threw them in. The shoes gleamed, tendrils of smoke wisped through the shoelace holes. He took off his woolen socks, threw them in too, and stared dully into the fire. His chest shone pink, and the wishbone of his ribs moved up and down as he gasped for breath. I too was mesmerized by the deep flames shot through with yellow-white streaks. Orange sparks spinning in his hair, my uncle took several steps closer.

"Uncle Tom!" I shrieked. "Stop!"

He did not hear. He kept walking, elbows bent, hands cupped in the wavering air. I threw my arms around his waist, but he was too strong and pried my fingers from his belt loops. Then I gave his shin a good, hard kick. He gasped and stumbled. I kicked again, this time aiming for the skinny tendon over his ankle. He sank to his knees, startled. Once more I pushed my toe into his calf, and he rolled to the side, safely out of danger.

Standing over him, I felt sick and strong at the same time. He offered me a weak smile. "It's all right, dear," he whispered. "I'm quite fine now."

"I better get Aunt Inez."

His fingers grabbed my sleeve. "No! Don't do that. Promise?"

I hesitated until I saw small teardrops on his lashes. As I listened to the crackle of things burning, I vowed never to tell anyone what I'd seen.

That night I dreamed my father and I stood on Horsendon Hill. Sudbury lay under a sheet of silvery water. The rest of my family was gathered on the deck of a ship. I knew this was the ship Aunt Inez had sailed on to come to England.

"Follow me, Meggie!" my father called. Then he spread his arms wide and hurled himself into the sea. Waves crashed around his shoulders as he swam toward the horizon.

"Daddy!" I shouted, and threw myself after him. A huge wave rolled behind me. I struggled to reach my father, only I was too slow and a ruffle of foam caught my chin. The boat was shrinking into the horizon, and Uncle Tom and George were growing smaller on the deck. The wave struck the back of my head, and I toppled forward into cold water, flooded with a darkness so complete I thought I was dead.

When I woke, I climbed out of bed, tiptoed to the window, and leaned outside. Quiet lay thick around me. In the garden corner, a small cone-shaped fire still glowed. A feather brushed my cheek. I looked up. A shower of sparks burst in the sky. The air seemed filled with water and ash. I remembered my dream of the ocean, the story of my grandmother weeping on the stairs, and Aunt Inez's jump into the English Channel. I saw the flames blaze higher and knew that the dirty, rough hunger in all of us would always burn, as it was carried down to George and me, who would always hold our hands open, needing to fill a hurt that began long before.

Ashes still fell. I could imagine them falling all night on the Sudbury rooftops, dusting the thin-petaled roses, smudging the red pillar boxes and double-deckers. They scattered all over England, lay silted between the pebbles of Brighton Beach, where they were drawn into the cloudy green Atlantic to New York, and down farther, to meet a delta of clear blue, while more ashes kept falling, as if the fire would never be put out.

Look into the sky and see the dimpled marks of those who have gone before. Those who have tracked across hills gentle as these, to find the secret fire of the universe. See their singed, ragged trails. The fire stuns everyone into silence. Still, they keep asking, "What is this substance called Light?"

Time is round. Turn it like a marble in your mind. Years swirl into ocean blue, seconds trapped in a milky breath. Look closer. Listen to the voices of those who have talked to the sky. See a sage named Uddalaka and his curious son, Svetaketu, roam a forest, asking questions. "Please, sir," the son asks one night, "what is the self?"

The father orders his son to pluck a fruit from the Nyagrodha tree. When he breaks it open, he asks him what he sees.

"I see some seeds."

"Break those open too."

"But there's nothing here!"

"The subtle essence you do not see, that is the whole of the Nyagrodha tree. In that, all things have their existence. And that is the ultimate truth."

The sky is now a great fruit, dripping its golden nectar to the earth. Star-shaped seeds hang in liquid pulp. Nothing can exist without this miraculous substance. Leaves unfurl, melons plump out. We cannot see anything, not the trees, not a crow lifting off a branch, not the shadows that move beneath. If we can know what light is, we can know the very essence of the universe.

Centuries pass. The earth, once flat, spins into a globe. Kepler sets it on an elliptical course. Galileo tilts his winking lantern from a hill, tries to measure the speed of a beam.

In a city of ice, a group of men in long coats huddle before this same glowing fruit. They too break it open to the smallest possible pieces. They lean their heads together, confer among themselves. One points this way, another that. Some men find a spitting seed that gouges a hole in a fine screen. Others see the ghostly smear of juice. Their voices clash in the wintry air. They want to tear each other's collars. But these are reasonable men, in search of reasonable answers.

"Let us agree," they say, "that Light is both."

And so in 1927, in a different city, a city of lace and chocolate, it is proclaimed that Light is both particle and wave, seed and juice, pebble and water, stone and ocean.

Jumbee Curse

There's a saying about Indians like my grandfather who voyaged to the Caribbean in the nineteenth century: Gone to Tapu. It means Gone to the Islands. It also means Disappeared. The folks who gathered their wooden feeding bowls, their rupees and chappals, and trudged onto the huge English boats couldn't think too much about a return. In their world, if you traveled west of the Indus River, you were lost to everyone back in India.

Often I think there are other ways to be lost, to fall off the edge. Just by not knowing the people closest to you.

Our family in England was like a small box, surrounded by a deep purple space I always wanted to leap into. In this space, which circled like a wilderness, were the stories of our shared family past—Guyana; the hot, drowsy sun; tales of madness; the family friends who'd disappeared to Toronto and New York; my aunts and uncle who still lived in our old house but whom we never visited.

When my parents were first married, my father took my mother down to Guyana to visit his family. Once there, she saw that my grandmother had bound her daughters to herself with a red ribbon. The sisters were so pleased by their brother's new, fair-skinned wife that they spun out the red ribbon and tied it sweetly around my mother's wrist. In this way, they turned my mother into another sister, so my father's generosity to her would spill all over them too. He would have to keep his promise.

Now that she was tied to the other women, my mother could not wander very far. Every time she tried to explore beyond the bounds of the house and yard, the sisters would feel a tug on the ribbon and jerk my mother back inside. They kept her close to them, so as not to disturb my father in his separate bedroom. My mother was miserable, always attached to the family.

In secret, she added another length of ribbon. When no one was looking, she could go as far as she pleased. She wandered the muddy roads and got to know the neighbors and local tailors and fruitsellers. At night, she visited my father in his little room of studying. There, she told me, one night a bird came and nested in her belly. That was me, her new baby. I pecked and pulled at the ribbon that now rubbed my mother's wrist raw. I let her take wing so she could finally leave Guyana. When we flew away, the red ribbon snapped. Blood fell everywhere, all over the faces of my aunts, all over the family house.

The Professor *of* Light

———

This is how I knew I was born in the blood of leaving. My family was lost to me, fallen off a dark edge. Yet I could not help imagining what lay over there, on the other side. If I shut my eyes, our family's house back in Guyana, built by Grandfather, burned terrible as a dream, as if I'd lived there myself; it squatted like a fat gull in the mud with its wide belly of a porch and two splintered wings.

I saw the tall French windows that faced east, six small children's bedrooms in a row, and a chicken coop kept in the bottomhouse, as the dank space under the stilts was called. Our house was the first in the village to change from kerosene to electricity, and the first again to get a shower stall. Sometimes my grandmother dressed her children in starched white clothes for services at the Presbyterian church. Other times she spread white petals on the floor of my father's room so she could read the footsteps of the ghosts that trod through the house at night.

In all the family stories I could hear the other, darker Guyana—the roads that flooded in the rainy season and would not drain, the broken-down shacks, and the rum house where Grandfather used to drink and gamble. In Guyana, something pulled from below. A lost ambition, a slow going backward. My father spoke in sorrowful tones of the relatives who stayed behind, as if they had buried themselves in the old cane fields.

Every couple of months, blue aerograms from Guyana would arrive, almost always carrying a plea for money. Auntie Edith, who had become a missionary for the local church, was the only one who earned a wage, and that was never enough. My father would slit open the glued edges and read the letter several times, his eyes slowly fogging over. Eventually he went upstairs and dashed off a check to his family. Sometimes he became so upset he would tear the letter up, and later I would find transparent blue bits under my parents' bed.

One afternoon, the summer I was eleven, a baby sparrow fell from its nest in Uncle Tom's chestnut tree. Aunt Inez came running when she heard my shout. We both stared at the broken-necked bird, pale as an eel, smashed on the pavement. "That's bad luck," she declared. She bent down and scooped it into her salmon-colored palms. "Its own family bring it down." She nodded to me. "Meggie, go get Uncle Tom's spade."

I went into the shed, where I pulled the spade out from under a bag of peat moss. Aunt Inez waited by the steps, the baby bird balanced inside the tent of her apron. Together we began to dig. Then she let the bird tumble into the hole. "A dead baby bird is the same as a lost child. If it's not taken care of properly, during a high wind it returns and comes to torment you." She added, "That's what happened with your uncle Joseph."

"Tell me."

"Oh, Meggie," she said. "Why you always want to hear those old stories? It's not nice to talk about the family back there."

"It's my family too," I insisted.

My aunt glanced down the alley between the shed and the side of the house. "All right, I'll tell you. But you mustn't say a word about this to anyone. Tom hates when I go on about the past."

"I promise."

She settled on the steps, and smoothed her apron over her knees. "Your uncle Joseph was so brilliant, the first boy in the whole Lettur Kenny village to pass his overseas exam. Everyone said Joseph was going to one day be a big and famous man. He went and got himself a job in the government, pretty high up."

Aunt Inez's face brimmed with pride, as when she boasted about my father and his accomplishments. "He did so well," she went on, "he got another job on a government base in Aruba. Now, your grandmother wasn't too happy about this. She sent him letters every week, begging him to come back home. He used to carry her letters in his pockets until they became heavy, like stones, and his feet start to drag. Soon he could not do his work in Aruba. He pack up his things and come home to us in Lettur Kenny."

She paused. A wild sadness showed in her face now. Her skin was melting-soft, her eyes wet black.

"What happened?" I asked.

"Something was wrong." She shook her head and dabbed a corner of an eye. "Poor Joseph complained about a funny noise in his head. He walked around the house talking to himself. One day he put on a suit and tie and went for a walk. He didn't come back for a whole two weeks. When he did, he could not even say where he'd been. He sat on the verandah and talk about the birds in his head."

My aunt's breaths were short and hard. Her fingers fumbled with the edge of her apron. "Soon he stopped talking altogether. Every time someone walk through the gate, he dart inside and hide in the shadows. He stayed for a few weeks and left to go wandering the countryside. That's what he came to do all the time. To this day, once a month, your auntie Edith and auntie

Didi dress him up in his nice white suit and drive him to the government office where he pick up his pension check, and they drive him back. He never spoke again. In Lettur Kenny we call it the jumbee curse."

"What does that mean?"

Her voice dropped to a low whisper, as if we were together in the bottomhouse, listening to family noises, the sound of Uncle Joseph walking on the floorboards overhead. "They say that every season when the old folks plant their seed cane in the fields, they remember their lost homes in India and weep tears of longing, which mingle in the earth. The rum they brew muddles their children's heads and makes them slow-footed and melancholy, so they can never leave home.

"Everyone says that the boys from Lettur Kenny village walk under a jumbee curse that comes from their families. They mixed up too much ambition and history in the boys' heads. That way they don't know if they want to go forward or back."

My aunt's gaze was fixed on a distant point over the garden fence. She was no longer in Guyana, but was standing on Brighton's pebbled shore, the old memories lapping inside her, until she grew afraid they might pull her under. Suddenly she stood, spine stiff, kicked some dirt over the hole we had dug, and said, "That's enough, Meggie. Too much of this talk and it brings you down. We living here now. And that's where we got to stay."

I didn't know what to believe about Guyana or my father or the jumbee curse. Whenever I thought of him and Joseph and those he'd grown up with, I saw these little boys walking along the muddy roads with enormous heads they could not carry on their shoulders. I liked to imagine that my father and I had taken our own boat and were sailing on the ocean to Guyana. His head was propped on his lap, huge as a flaming orange pumpkin, as he talked to me about the meaning of light.

On and on he went about the crazy, infinite energy of the universe, how he and I could be sitting in a thousand other boats on a thousand other seas. The ocean swelled and tilted, pulled our boat toward the equator, which to me was the edge of the world, where everything fell off.

I often wondered why we didn't spend more time with the other men who had taken boats and airplanes and landed in America and England to find work and apparently could carry their heads just fine. But what about Uncle Joseph, whose head grew too heavy and who stayed behind?

"I loved my brother so much," my father told me when I asked him. "Joseph was the one who taught me how to think like a philosopher. We used to sit on our verandah, and he would say, 'See that brier tree? How we know that tree exists?' "

I giggled, thrilled that my father had asked questions in Guyana, years before, just as he and I did at home and in England. It made me feel that there was another ribbon, braided out of talk and stories, that tied the family to me.

"Do you miss him?" I asked.

He hesitated. "No matter how much I love my brother, we can't stay in the past. I remember what he taught me about a man named Descartes. The self builds up knowledge. The self can do anything. And that's what we got to do. We got to pick up our selves and start new again. We try to become what we can."

I kept pondering what my father said about the self and moving on. If I was born in the blood of leaving, what was the self that carried on? What part of me changed, and what stayed the same?

Since we arrived in Sudbury this summer, more and more of my father's old self started showing. After breakfast every morning he swung out of the gate and called to neighbors, like a boy ambling down the road. When he returned, he worked at a folding table in the garden. His latest chapter was going very well, he told me, for he was writing about Descartes, and he often recalled the long talks he and Joseph used to have on the verandah.

He even began to reminisce about his friends in Lettur Kenny, the cricket games he used to play. "All those years in college and graduate school, and I work so hard I never have a chance to see them," he mused. "Maybe I should give some of those fellows a call."

"And why you want to do that for?" Aunt Inez asked. "Those boys are lazy. They don't know how to get on with their lives."

Aunt Inez didn't approve of Guyanese anymore. She thought them lax and deceitful, and hated how they wore their shirts open to show their black curly chest hair. Every now and then she softened, though. One evening she agreed to go to a party at the house of some Guyanese my family knew in the Berbice, the region they were from. George and I sat in a corner of the garden and made fun of the other kids. Gold chains gleamed on the boys' necks, and they wore polyester shirts unbuttoned at the chest and too tight hiphugger pants. The girls were in frilly dresses that shushed when they moved their hips to dance. To us, they were funny immigrants, greased down in bad taste.

"That's the last time I'll do something like that," Aunt Inez fumed on the ride home.

My father protested. "But it was so sweet. Like no time has passed."

"That's my point!" Aunt Inez countered. "Time never move on with those folks."

Aunt Inez did approve of one of my father's friends, Arun Bannerjee. Dr. Bannerjee, as she called him, ranked very high in her mind. He was Indian Indian, taught in the same department as my father at college, and had won a prestigious fellowship to Cambridge University. When he came to visit at my aunt and uncle's, he slipped his sandals off in the entry hall and politely turned down a lunch of beef stew; this refusal impressed my aunt for its moral purity.

Back in the States, we didn't see the Bannerjees very much. My mother claimed they were snobs and that Mrs. Bannerjee gave her nasty looks because she didn't go to their parties dressed up in a sari like the other wives. Even though the Bannerjees lived a few blocks away from us, their daughter Nila, who was a year younger than I, hung around only with other Indian kids who liked to dance to old Hindi film songs.

Arun was a small man with a nose that bent to his lips, which made me think he was always sniffing the fragrance of his own ideas since he loved them so much. Everyone said Arun was brilliant; he knew all about politics and history and philosophy. During that visit he enthused about the splendid library at

Cambridge and his brilliant colleagues there, and urged my father to apply for the same fellowship he had won. "I'm sure the department would be very interested in your research," he said.

My father's eyebrows rose. "Me?"

"And why not?" Arun passed a hand through his hair. I didn't like his hair. Unlike my father's, which flopped in wild waves around his brow, Arun's lay flat and brushed into a smooth line. His fingers also bothered me. They were thin and delicate, as if he did not like to touch anything but himself. "Don't you think Uncle Warren should make a go of it?" he asked Nila.

"Sure." She grinned at me. A flower-shaped stud, each petal a different color, sparkled in her nose. "It's really fun there."

Arun made a few phone calls on my father's behalf and arranged for him to give a lecture at a nearby library. As it turned out, a Dr. Whyte who lived in Sudbury had attended Cambridge, and his wife ran the local cultural series.

On a Thursday, I accompanied my father to the library, a lovely Tudor building set in a garden. My father decided to hold his talk outside, and led a line of blue-haired ladies down the slate paths, past the neat rows of violet- and yellow-petaled flowers, until he stopped at a large round bed of petunias.

"Imagine this is the universe," he said, pointing. "All the planets and stars are the twigs and pebbles stuck inside the moist ground. That's what we call the plenum. Every time it rains, the water trickles down through the cracks in the dirt.

"According to Descartes, light is something that wants to trickle out, something that has to move." He pinched my ear. "Just like my daughter here. She moves so fast I can't keep up!"

I could see many of the women break into smiles. Then they gathered in a knot as he cajoled them about philosophy. Afterward, Mrs. Whyte, the woman in charge, rushed up to my father and squeezed his arm. "Dr. Bannerjee was so right, you are a wonderful speaker. It's too late to get out the publicity for a proper series. But next summer you must give us a lecture every week."

"If you like," my father said, taking an embarrassed step backward.

She squeezed his arm and held her hand there. "I won't have anything less."

I didn't particularly like this woman, with her American and British accents wobbling around in her horsey mouth, but my father was obviously flattered. When we turned to walk home, he took my hand and said, "You see, Meggie? Now you understand why I don't look back to my brother Joseph. I've found a better brother in a man like Arun."

Arun Bannerjee wasn't our only visitor that summer. Sheila Pereira came to stay with us, bringing news of all the people my father had lost touch with in Guyana. A second cousin of my father and my aunt's, Sheila grew up across the road in Lettur Kenny and moved to Georgetown when she was sixteen. "She gone Casablanca," the family often said of her, which meant she was a girl who went with a fast city crowd and did as she pleased. At nineteen she ran away with a rich Brazilian businessman, whom we never saw. She breezed through London every few months and stayed with us in Sudbury for a couple of weeks before moving on.

"It's the Punjabi princess," my aunt declared when she arrived this time. She sniffed at Sheila's tailored tweed suits, pockets hung with loops of gold chain. I could not take my eyes off Sheila; her skin was a smooth teak, her waist perfect. She gave me an idea of what I might look like when I grew up, since I did not resemble my own mother, with her green eyes and freckled arms.

Sheila brought me a red velvet vest, woven with silk arabesques and studded with sequin mirrors. The vest was given to her, she explained, by an Air-India pilot who occasionally arrived in London to sweep her up and take her to places such as Bombay or somewhere on the Horn of Africa. He would call at all hours of the night. My aunt and uncle didn't know his name, exactly, for he always chimed out something like, "Moobie"—or Boomboom—"here, calling from Dubai. Can you put Sheila on?"

A few months before, Sheila told us, the pilot's family had arranged a bride for him, which meant Sheila and he would not be able to see each other—at least not as easily. The last time he saw Sheila, he bestowed on her this beautiful vest. He told her that each sequin was for a country he had flown over to be with her. By now, though, Sheila felt quite done with her pilot—that's why she gave the vest to me.

"That woman is downright vulgar," my aunt scoffed after Sheila went upstairs to unpack.

"Leave her alone," my father said. "She come here and give us a taste of all the folk we done forgot."

Aunt Inez banged into the kitchen to make us supper, saying, "That's one taste I don't need in my mouth!"

But she couldn't have been too mad at my father for his homesickness, because that night she made us a huge pot of chicken curry. When my father scooped up meat between his fingers, she tapped her fork on her plate. "That's uncivilized," she said.

Sheila leaned back in her chair, a small, mirthful expression on her lips, and said to my father, "Look here, dear. You really ought to give some of the old boys a ring. There's some fellows living right down the road. You can't lose touch altogether, you know."

After lunch the next day my father dialed the numbers Sheila had given him. "Yes, man, it's the book boy, ready to lift his head up," I heard him say, and soon he was bellowing with jokes, catching up with the village boys he'd lost track of.

I grew excited as I imagined these strange men jumping to life like characters in a dream story. They were even real enough to invite my father to a cricket game later that afternoon.

"What do you want to do that for?" my aunt asked when he told her he'd be going. She and Uncle Tom were getting ready to visit a sick friend on the other side of town; she had put on a mulberry wool dress, Sunday hat pulled over her curls. Though George hated trips like this, he meekly agreed to go along. After last summer, when he was punished for running too much water in the tub and setting the fire, George didn't stick too close to me, particularly when there might be some mischief afoot. He'd grown a little afraid of my family and the possibilities that might spark between us.

"Warren likes to play cricket," my mother said. "Now he can meet up with some old friends."

"Old friends," Aunt Inez grumbled. "I know all those rum-headed fellows. You watch, if you invite them over, the first thing they do is they going to ask us for money. They come back like ghosts, all the time."

"Oh, Inez. You are too much sometimes. You forget you were an immigrant once too."

"Forget!" She tugged on her gloves, grabbed George and Timmy by their hands, and patted Uncle Tom on the arm. "I made a good life for myself here. I didn't come to England to listen to their stories and moan about the old country. I married a good man." She opened the door, and as she flounced through the gate, she shouted over her shoulder, "No visitors!"

The moment Aunt Inez left, the house took on a different, careless air. Anything was possible. I zigzagged through the rooms, thrilled by the bright spangles that danced off my vest. The lunch dishes were left undone. Instead of folding the laundry, which lay in crumpled heaps on the chairs in the back parlor, my mother and Sheila opened Sheila's suitcase. Inside were dozens of shalwar kamizes and saris the Air-India pilot had given her. Out they poured, a stream of riotous color—pink chiffon dupattas, sea-blue saris flecked with gold. Near the dusty grays and blues of Aunt Inez's blouses, they looked tempting as a meal. I wanted to dive inside, nuzzle in the buttery yellows and creamy browns. I pressed a cotton print kurta with a tassel of cork buttons to my face, and sniffed its mysterious, woody scent.

My mother and Sheila were already putting on outfits and displaying them for each other. My mother wore a lime-colored shalwar, a deep-orange dupatta running down her back in an extravagant flame. Sheila modeled a slinky silk kurta with matching harem-style pants that gapped open and gave quick glimpses of her slender thighs.

Then they lounged in the garden with lemon slices on their eyes and sipped spiked iced tea, while I sat at their feet. My mother and Sheila seemed to have forgotten about Aunt Inez, the dirty dishes, and the wash.

A few hours later, my father burst through the door in a swell of chatter. I had never seen him like this. His Caribbean dialect had fully returned in those few hours away, like a musical record he'd kept locked and unplayed in a closet. "Look it here!" he greeted my mother. "This here Maywa and Charles, they second cousins of mine and now they living in England!"

Charles was golden-skinned; his round bald head shone like an upturned brass pot. Creases etched the corners of his mouth. Although I was glad they were here, I imagined Charles's voice sweeping through the room like a noisy wind, toppling my aunt's nice things.

Quickly my mother scooped the bright-colored clothes onto the chairs, then followed the men into the front parlor. Behind her, Sheila, eyes flashing, pushed the hair from her brow. "You boys play all day and forget about the girls at home, hunh?" Sheila's accent also seemed suddenly thicker, saucy with teasing.

"Now Sheila," Charles answered, "how we stay away, knowin' you beautiful women waitin' here?" He turned to the others. "Besides, you think we can play one of those games whole day long? They interminable, man, interminable!"

My father had gone to a corner of the front parlor, where he took liquor bottles from the cabinet. "What'll it be?" he called out. "Whiskey, gin, rum?"

I remembered Aunt Inez's disapproving glare when she'd

left in a huff that morning. "We're not supposed to open the liquor cabinet. Aunt Inez said."

"Oh, Megan," my mother chided. "Stop repeating what adults say."

"Listen to that!" Sheila teased. "Meggie got a touch of Inez's starch in her!"

"Don't worry, little lady. Just a nip to get everyone going." My father winked at me.

"Going where?" my mother asked, though the smile on her face showed she was pleased. After all, if liquor flowed, the more exciting the talk, and the more interesting the evening.

My father's laughter rumbled in the room. "I cannot believe it! I look over the other team, and who is there but that old clown Charles! And Maywa, you used to climb the coconut trees, man, faster than a rat."

"Not anymore." Maywa rubbed his kneecap. "I'm a serious fellow, Warren. Just like you. I'm going to be a doctor."

I could not keep from looking at Maywa, for he looked like someone I already knew. I wondered if Uncle Joseph looked like him, with his rail-thin body, his trouser hems that reached only to the bony knobs of his ankles. I watched Maywa pace between the sofa and chairs, unable to settle down. Finally he picked up Uncle Tom's porcelain miniatures of London Bridge and Big Ben, and put them in a different place. He stopped moving only when my father handed him a glass of rum, which he drank in long, noisy gulps.

"I know Charles since we were babies," my father explained. "Our mothers, they like sisters."

"What you saying, man?" Charles countered. "Your side of the family so proud, it don't talk to mine!"

Maywa lifted his face from his glass and grinned. "Charles, you makin' up stories. It my side of the family they pass on the road and turn their heads away. They think we too common and stupid."

"That is the damn blasted truth," Charles agreed.

Sheila pranced around the room like a pretty colt, fist on a hip, while the men watched admiringly. "And why he not pass you on the road!" she exclaimed. "He got better things to do than hang with you slow-movin' boy! I'd pass you on the road too, and never come back!"

"Oh, Sheila, you gone pass us long ago." Maywa pretended to grab his chest, heartsick. Smirking, Sheila sashayed out of the room to help my mother in the kitchen.

Drinks were poured again and the conversation churned on. The room filled with a yellow warmth, the men's voices swirls and eddies that I wanted to swim inside. I grew dizzy trying to follow what was being said. Every time someone asserted something, it was loudly and vehemently contradicted by someone else. I had the feeling some kind of joke was being made among them. But no matter how hard I listened, I couldn't get it. I longed to run across the room, lean into the round of my father's stomach, join him while he traveled into the memories of Guyana.

My mother returned to the front parlor with a tray of sandwiches and pushed past the men's sprawled legs. Her dupatta bounced against her back, so everyone had to pay attention to her. "I hope this will do," she said. "My sister-in-law doesn't keep much in the way of Indian food in the house." The men murmured their thanks and took the sandwiches. Maywa's teeth flashed, small and sharp, against his dark skin.

Charles was the loudest by now. "Come, Meggie, come!" he bellowed. "Talk to Uncle Charles." He made gobbling noises in his throat and swung his arms out like tentacles.

They're making fun of me, I thought, and shrank against the wall, glaring at these strange men, who now seemed so foreign. Charles waved insistently. "You come to Guyana, child, and we drive a jeep, how you like that? We drive a jeep very fast to the jungle and Kaieteur Falls. You know we got the tallest falls in the world there?"

"I thought Niagara Falls were," I replied, and stroked my vest, which felt like shiny armor. The gold brocade rubbed rough and stiff against my bare arms, and I noticed a few sequins fall to the rug.

Maywa downed the last of his drink, and cocked his head at me. "She half Indian," he said. "I can tell."

"She look a little like Warren's sister Didi, don't you think?" Sheila asked. "So pretty."

"She better have more brains, then!" Charles said.

"What she need brains for?" Maywa sneered. He stared at his empty glass. "She a girl!"

My mother reddened and my father wagged a finger in my direction. "You watch what you say. My daughter going to tell you the longitude and latitude of Kaieteur Falls and how old a fool you are! This little girl going to pass us all by one day."

Everybody roared with laughter, which I thought idiotic, for Charles especially. I remembered everything Aunt Inez had said about the Guyanese, how lax and coarse their humor was.

Maywa chewed a sandwich as if the talk had made him hungry. When he finished, he licked his fingers and nodded.

"It's hard, man, comin' over here. But you doing good, man. Inez's husband own this house? And you folks come to England every year? You must make a good salary. You go Yankee up all right."

"We do fine." My mother's voice was brittle and nervous.

"You stop your bellyachin' and you go Yankee up too," Sheila said.

My father, Charles, and Sheila burst out laughing. Only Maywa didn't seem to enjoy the joke. He hunched over his knees, his shoulder blades two jutting wings. A disgruntled air settled on the room when everyone saw how angry he was.

I could tell from the grin taking hold on my father's face that a story was brewing inside him. Whenever things turned uncomfortable in a room, my father came up with a story that was meant to make everyone feel better. His black eyes shone with a mysterious innocence as he began his story.

"When I was boy, I was just like my daughter Meggie here, always asking so many questions. One day I walking to school when a man stop me in the road."

"I remember that walk," Charles interjected. "Mrs. Persaud use to call from the verandah, ask us to buy a tin of milk for her because her feet achin'—"

"No, no, that's Mrs. Bacchus, she always moanin' about her no-good son never help her out—" Maywa offered.

"I roundin' the road by Mrs. Persaud's," my father went on, "when this man say to me, 'Boy, I seen your brother Joseph lyin' in the ditch.' I say, 'Bring me to him.' The man just smile and say, 'You give me a dollar first and I show you.' I get so mad, I stamp my feet and threaten to turn this bloody fool over to the authorities."

"Authorities!" Charles scoffed. "You talkin' about that Rama-swamy fellow hang a Justice of the Peace sign and charge every-one a fast dollar—"

The people and houses they mentioned sprang up in my mind, vivid as a movie screen. The men talked as if they were walking on the village roads, feeling the sun on their backs right now.

My father easily picked up where he left off, for the detours seemed part of the story too. "This fellow got a Ramaswamy crafty face. He just look at me and say, 'Boy! The judge, he my brother!' So I set down on the side of the road to think. I look at my clean hands. His hands dirty. I say to him, 'You know who I am?' The man say, 'Your name Warren Singh.'

" 'That's correct,' I say to him. 'You know who else I am?'"

"The man, he get nervous. 'I'm from the Singh family, the house that catch jumbee,' I tell him. Then I grab his dirty hand and read his palm. You know I read palms, right? Maybe I do it for you later—"

"Daddy, get to the point!" I cried.

"Okay, okay. So I show him the traces on his lifeline and tell him he have either misfortune or luck up ahead, depending on how good he is in life. All those traces, they dirt, they not lines at all. He believe me, though. I make a lot of sorry sounds. 'Your luck turning bad as we speak,' I tell him. The fellow get so scared he drag me to a field where Joseph sleeping dead drunk in a hole in the ground."

"What you do then?" Charles asked.

"First I stand over my brother, hit my hands together and say all kinda mumbo-jumbo. Then I leave Joseph there. Better he get a crick in his neck and feel sorry when he wake. The man, he run away in fright, think I put a curse on my brother. Stupid fellow."

"That's good, I like that!" Charles clapped a hand on my father's shoulder. "Warren always clever. That's why he an American professor and we all just bums fresh off the boat, huh?"

My father's confident, booming voice drained from the room. Charles and Maywa quietly sipped their drinks. I noticed how dark it was outside. Circles of car headlights bloomed through the curtains, then sank into the evening shadows. My mother walked to the bay window and parted the curtains. Aunt Inez had not called; this might or might not mean she would return any minute. My stomach began to hurt when I thought of the unfolded wash and clothes in the back parlor, our guests sprawled on the chairs. The darkness seemed to descend more swiftly, and I wondered how much longer Charles and Maywa could possibly stay.

As my mother returned to her stool, something was wrong. We noticed a low noise, like a small animal growling in a bush. I turned my eyes to Maywa. Long legs stretched out, he had slid down in his seat and was muttering a string of words that made no sense. Gently Charles tapped my father on the shoulder, and they left the room.

"How long have you been here?" my mother asked Maywa in a bright voice.

His head lolled back, and he regarded her with glazed, half-shut eyes. "I study in Georgetown. Medicine. I not so lucky, like your husband. I come here and work on lorry, now I sell pharmaceuticals." His sentences shifted into a slow, furious rhythm. "I study medicine, now I work. Sell pharmaceuticals."

My mother got up to leave, and Sheila followed, picking up

the dirty glasses. "Excuse us, please," my mother said. "We've got to begin supper." Maywa didn't respond.

I felt bad being left with Maywa and his strange noises, for I was missing out on what was really going on. And sure enough, I could hear angry voices down the hall. "Just a little favor, man!" I heard Charles yell. "It don't cost anything in the end!"

Maywa sat up, tense and alert. Aunt Inez had been right, after all. They just wanted money. But as I stared at Maywa, I couldn't help feeling that she was wrong too. There was something sad and beautiful in his face. The muscles in his slender neck strained as he tried to hear every word on the other side of the wall. He made me think of a long slim horse pushing at a wire fence. When a door slammed shut somewhere in the house, his whole body trembled.

"Are you really going to be a doctor?" I asked. If I could put a finger on the velvety skin on his neck, I thought, I might understand what he truly wanted, and who these people were to us.

Maywa's head slowly rotated in my direction. "You don't believe your uncle Maywa?"

"You're not my uncle."

"Everyone your relative, child," he said softly. "Everyone related."

He made me feel ashamed for being mistrustful. But before I could utter another word, he had jerked toward the door as my mother's voice broke through the others. "I heard that talk in the parlor before! You think we're rich just because we live in the States? You want us to give away the little we have?"

"Not give!" Maywa shouted at the closed door, and flung it

open. Behind me, the porcelain miniatures thudded on the rug. Maywa ran down the hall, shouting, "You don't have to *give* anything!"

In the back parlor, Charles, his once shiny face now dull with anger, stood next to the table. "It's all very simple and straightforward," he was saying. But what he went on to say didn't seem simple at all. Again and again he ran over complicated routes for getting money out of Guyana, so Maywa could go to medical school rather than work selling pharmaceuticals.

A crucial step in this scheme had something to do with my father's bank account in the States. Whenever this was mentioned, my mother's voice rang out, hot and forceful: "That money is our hard-earned savings, and we certainly aren't going to part with it!"

I too felt a surge of pride and resentment. I could see the quarters and dollar bills stacked up in a silver box and these awful men snatching them away. I didn't understand. Did she or didn't she like them?

Sheila stood between the two groups. "You all have to stop fighting now," she said. "You know each other since you children, you can't be carryin' on like this!"

Maywa turned to her, his face swollen with rage. "What you sayin' with your fancy clothes and that high look on your face, Casablanca girl? So you marry up! Is all the same!"

"Maywa," Charles warned.

"Don't you stop me, man. Is true! All of you, high-up girls, lookin' down on us poor boys. Who you to sneer?"

Charles shoved Maywa in the arm. "Maywa, you watch what you say. We don't talk like that here."

Maywa dropped to a seat. "Forget it, man," he said. "Forget we asked."

My father, quietly pouring drinks at the other end of the table, put the cap back on the whiskey bottle. He looked relieved as he announced, "Here you go! One more round to warm you up!" As he pushed the glasses across the tablecloth, I had the sense he was pushing himself away too, making bigger the distance between himself and the other men.

Before Charles and Maywa could reach for their drinks, though, the strangest thing happened. Maywa tore off his cricket sweater, threw it on the floor, raised his arms and began to flap them. He circled the room, swooped into furniture like a gangly bird. "Ya-eeeh!" he shouted. I watched him thrash the air, listened to the tick of his fingernails as they struck a lampshade, the edge of a picture frame. Is this a jumbee bird, I wondered. One of his hands caught on a dupatta draped across a chair, and it streaked across the room like a puff of blue wind.

"Maywa!" Charles cried. "What you doing now!"

Maywa was already nearing the kitchen door. "Work now, sell pharmaceuticals," he chanted, and wrenched it open. "Pharmaceuticals!" he yelled into the night air.

We crammed through the narrow doorway and onto the steps to watch Maywa race around the darkened garden, trip over flower beds, thrust his skinny arms into the strips of wash. "Doctor!" he kept shouting. "I going to be a doctor!" When he found himself wrapped in a cowl of sheets, with a cry he tore them off and swerved toward the low shadows of rosebushes.

"Damn him," Charles said. "The fool's going to get himself pricked."

"That fool is drunk," my father added.

Sheila's fingers lightly touched my cheek. "That boy hurt himself more than he hurt any of us."

We watched as Maywa hurtled through the garden. He would swerve out of danger as each new obstacle appeared—the rubbish pile, Uncle Tom's wheelbarrow and tools. I heard his shin bone hit brick as he stumbled forward.

Charles winced and stepped from the porch as Maywa halted a few feet away, sweat pouring down his face. He tipped forward, arms raised, then flung himself on the ground with a dead, moist thump, as if hugging the earth to his chest.

"Is he all right?" my mother asked.

"He's fine," Charles said. "Just actin' up like the crazy fellow he was in Lettur Kenny."

"Oh, you boys." Sheila's voice was tinged with regret. "We better get him out of here before Inez come back."

We hurried down the steps and gathered to stare at his long, broken shape in the grass. When my mother spoke, it sounded as if she were crying. "I can't get over it," she said. "He looks so much like Joseph."

"Same hard head," Charles agreed, and added wistfully, "Same sadness inside."

My father touched his cousin's sleeve. "It all right." His voice was distant and hoarse. "Everything going to be all right now."

The air was cool. From the nearby station came the faint clacks of a passing train. It made me feel that Guyana and what they'd come from were not far away at all. I wondered if everyone else was thinking what I was; maybe Maywa had the jumbee curse too. The odor of diesel mingled with the sadness they were speaking of; I sensed it as the smoky weight of their memories, now mine. And for once I could travel inside the old places and see everything I wanted to know.

In the house, the phone was ringing. It was Aunt Inez, saying they would be home by nine-thirty, and to please leave the front porch lamp on. My mother heated the curry and rice left over from the night before. We were suddenly very hungry; it was a craving, an emptiness we had to fill. I had the sense, as Sheila lit two candles, that the grown-ups were trying to keep what was fast disappearing, the warm glow of trust among them, before it was gone again.

The room echoed with stories about Guyana and England and people I didn't know; their chatter left spaces in the air from so many mysteries. My stomach squeezed tight as the hands of the mantel clock edged toward nine-thirty.

My mother caught the squeak of the front gate, and we could all hear Aunt Inez on the front path as she told George to hurry up, stop dragging like that, she had a lot to do. Sheila stuffed her clothes into her suitcase and tamped down Aunt Inez's pile of blouses.

My mother got up from the table, and I saw Charles touch my father's shoulder and say quickly, "Tomorrow, Warren. Tomorrow we work out the details."

I put my fork down. I had missed a signal, some invisible agreement between them. I jumped onto my chair and shouted over the din, "Are you giving Maywa money?"

My mother shot my father a distressed look. "Warren, you promised—"

I didn't want them to start fighting. I wanted to know what was going on. "Daddy, tell me," I insisted.

My father pointed at me. "Megan, get down from there."

"Tell me!"

"I'm warning you, young lady! This is no way to behave!"

Aunt Inez's high voice sailed through the walls. "Who's here?" she called. "Who's come visiting at this hour?"

She pushed inside, her eyes wide as she took in the scene. "Charles? What you doing here? I knew it! I can't leave for one day, and my house is not my own!"

My knees began to tremble. "Tell me," I whimpered. "Does Maywa have the jumbee curse?"

"Jumbee curse! Is that what kind of talk is going on here?" Aunt Inez's hat bounced on her head as she marched into the room and swept an arm over the table, which was littered with capsized bottles and half-filled glasses. She held the rum bottle by its neck and waved it in the air. "Talkin' jumbee while my niece jumpin' like a fool bird on the good chair! Get down from there, young lady, and take off that ridiculous vest!"

I bent my head. All at once my vest looked garish and ugly.

My aunt glowered at my father. "And you, Warren! What you promisin' now?"

"Nothin', Inez," he said.

"And my clothes! My poor wrinkled blouses! What is all this?" She plunged her hands into a pink-and-blue shalwar, and tufts of silk and nylon cloth floated in the air.

Charles kept glancing at the kitchen door. I could see scrolled across his mind: Please don't Maywa come in now. But the ruffled curtains shook on their rods, the door gave an impertinent bang, and in lurched Maywa, roused from his sleep, hair wild. He lunged forward to groan, "Where the loo, man?"

Shocked, Aunt Inez let the shalwar fall from her fingers.

Uncle Tom appeared in the doorway, his face drawn.

"Loo, man!" Maywa moaned and grabbed his stomach. "Gotta go to the loo!"

Uncle Tom did not move. A hush fell on the room. Slowly, my uncle reached out both hands, as if begging the man who wove and swore before him like a belligerent spirit. Then I saw what lay in his palms, bright as bits of the moon: the porcelain miniatures of Big Ben and London Bridge, each broken cleanly in two.

Maywa and Charles didn't come back to visit. Sheila left a few days later for Paris, much to my aunt's relief. I wandered through the rooms, searching for the glimpse of Guyana I'd seen that night, just as I searched for the sequins that lay scattered in the rugs.

I did hear stories. Not long after Charles and Maywa's visit, while Maywa was making one of his pharmaceutical deliveries to a public clinic, he sneaked into an empty doctor's office. There he put on the doctor's white coat and fastened pens to his pocket. He told the patients waiting in the hallway that he was the new doctor, helping with the extra cases. Once in the examination room, he listened to their ailments, felt for the pulses in their bony wrists. On a prescription pad he scribbled the names of ointments and antibiotics, learned from the labels of cartons he regularly delivered. After some time the real doctor wondered what had happened to his patients. When he and the nurse opened the door, they found Maywa standing in front of a mirror, taking off the white lab coat, putting it on again, and taking it off again.

The authorities didn't put Maywa in jail but sent him to a psychiatric hospital for two weeks "for observation." We received letters from Maywa and Charles, which my father would read. According to them, the authorities had forgiven Maywa and said that if he could raise the money, he could go to medical school.

I often heard arguments behind closed doors. "That doctor talk is nonsense," my aunt told my father once. "You know those Guyanese boys. They never tell the truth. They can't help themselves." My mother agreed, though with a wistfulness in her voice, and I knew she was remembering the good time we had had that evening, before everything went wrong. "Maybe you should write them and say we're thinking about it," she told my father. Later I found the torn-up letters on the floor under his desk.

One evening, after another fight with my aunt, my father came downstairs to make a phone call. From the parlor I could hear his voice, though I couldn't tell what he was saying. When he returned, he said to me, "Come, Meggie. Come keep your old man company."

I was sad. The father who walked beside me was so tired he could barely hold up his shoulders. "It's hard being who I am," he confided. "The people from my past, they want so much. They want more than I can give."

In silence we crossed Greenford Avenue and hiked through the woods. The sun had set and the trees struck long poses against the sky. I thought of the nests sheltered in their branches, the baby birds with shrunken legs pulled against their fragile ribs. I shivered in my polo shirt and shorts.

"I used to take long walks like this when I was a little boy," he continued. "In Guyana the land is so beautiful at night, it goes for miles and miles, with the biggest sky you ever see. When there's no moon, you can't see anything. And the silence! That quiet can kill, Megan. If you listen, you can see and hear so much. If you're not afraid, you can understand things. The earth, it can talk to you."

"Aunt Inez told me that if you find a dead baby bird, you have to bury it in the ground or it will come back to haunt you."

"That's right," he said, putting his hand in mine. "They say when a high wind comes, you got to shout the names of lost children, otherwise they going to harm you."

"Were there lots of lost children in Guyana?"

"Some."

"Was my uncle Joseph lost, Daddy?"

"I tell you, Megan. It's not easy, growing up the way we did. The day each one of us children was born, my mother stick a knife in the door so we never leave her house. That's what the old folk did. They also send us to the Presbyterian school down the road, where we learn about the world outside our village. We learn you can be anything if you study hard enough. I believe them so much I used to sleep with a book under my pillow."

I giggled.

"Your uncle Joseph, he believed this too. He grew up to be a man of high thinking. But he could not stay away from the sound of my mother's voice. He could not hold everything inside him.

So he became a man with a bitter mouth, sitting on the verandah, talking away his big dreams until he could talk no more."

"I'm scared," I said. The dark seemed to press in at all sides; the birds might tumble out of their nests. "Uncle Joseph is going to hurt me."

"You mustn't be scared. You the one that going to carry us higher than we ever go. Why you scared?"

"Uncle Joseph is going to bring me down too."

"Oh, no. We can take care of that."

"How?"

"We going to shout your uncle's name."

"Really?"

"You bet."

Together, hands cupped over our mouths, we shouted into the air: "Joseph! Joseph!" Our voices soared over the trees, mingling in the air. My lungs filled with a strong wind that blew the lid of sky open. The tops of the trees trembled, the nests burned like garlands of fire until the sky spread into a banner of flames. I felt such strength and fiery power that I hardly noticed my father had led us to a small clearing in the woods.

Who should step out from behind a tree, slippery as a mist, but Maywa. He looked thinner than I remembered, bent and old. As he moved around a stump with an uneven jerk, I noticed the dark circles ringing his eyes. From his jacket my father drew out a blue envelope. Maywa's voice sputtered with gratitude as he stuffed it into his pocket. "You a good man, Warren. You don't forget." He reached for my father's shoulders, but my father danced sideways in embarrassment, saying, "That's okay, man. You get yourself settled, you hear?"

Left with his arms in the air, Maywa turned around. Before I could step away, he lifted me. His bristly chin rubbed my cheek, and he said, "I see you there, little girl. What you watching?"

"You." His hands pressed as though they might crush my spine into my rib cage.

"And what you see?"

"I see a man," I choked out.

"Not just any man, child. You see a doctor. A doctor who one day going to come back for you and take you to see Kaieteur Falls. We going to see the home that still shine so bright in your eyes."

I didn't like this Maywa. From between the spaces of his teeth drifted the yellow scent of rum. His eyes were the color of dead leaves that I feared I would lose myself in.

My father came forward. "That's enough now," he said. "Leave my girl alone. You must go."

Maywa squeezed me tighter, until I thought I was going to break apart, fall, and die smothered inside the loamy darkness of his eyes.

"Go!" my father ordered.

Maywa let go, and I dropped down, gasping. A moment later, the ground seemed to part and Maywa splintered into a thousand men, all stepping into the spaces between the trees until they had vanished like a thousand ghosts.

My father and I did not leave right away. We stared into the desolate forest, the shouts of before long gone from our throats. Leaves settled around our feet, smelling of Maywa. My father stroked my head. Not once, but several times, his palm brushed against my hair. It was as if he—maybe all the adults—were pushing something aside, hoping I could reach a far-off place he could not touch himself.

In Guyana light is all around. It tumbles, yellow and bright, from the huge flat sky. It falls on the green cane fields, burns the stooped backs of the men cutting cane. It catches like flames on the copper pots the women carry on their heads. And one day it fell through a schoolhouse window and turned a boy into light.

He was a melting-sweet boy who lived in a world where nothing stayed the same. Blazing sun peeled the white paint off flimsy houses, turned them into hollow bones flaked dry. Floods came, stilts buckled into mud. Palm fronds withered to threads of dust. Inside the shade of a verandah, the boy's brother rotted, his mind a mash of voices.

That day a ray of sun slanted through the window and stroked the boy's cheek. His skin tingled with warmth. He turned over his palm and saw its lines were roads, leading straight through the paper-thin walls. The schoolteacher's face was sand, his lashes a white dust. When he smiled, the air crumbled.

Soon the boy's head was filled with a pure brilliance that blotted everything out—the one-room schoolhouse, the teacher's stern mouth, the village boys sitting humble and quiet in their seats. He was melting into crystal waves that slid through the window, outside. He flew, straight to the sun, until he was scorched to weightless ash.

The boy was on the other side, where solid and liquid, light and shadow were no more. He swam inside the splendors of paradox. There were oranges without rind or flesh, oceans of atoms, hailstones of smoke. He was everywhere, curled into the crevice of a bark, bounced off a streetcar's window. He was glaring and loud, soft and subtle. Unbounded, he spread in timeless directions. He was the moon, the galaxies, a river's dark muscle.

A nasty voice broke his reverie, plunged him downward. His nose burrowed in the rank smell of dirt. In his mouth he tasted soot.

"Warren Singh!" the voice thundered, and something long and hard came crashing down on his knuckles. He let out a scream. A hot pain seared his hand.

The schoolmaster stood over him, wielding the flat of his ruler. "If you don't pay attention, young man, you'll be like your brother, sitting in the house, never making anything of yourself!"

The boy's vision was gone. He shrank against the school bench, cradling his throbbing hand. "You don't know what

*you're saying," he wanted to cry out. "You don't know what I've
seen!" But the schoolmaster had already turned his back.*

The next day, the boy found a book on his desk. Aristotle,
On the Heavens. *And another, on another day, Euclid,*
The Elements. *He loved the titles, their radiant promise.*
De Revolutionibus Orbium Coelestium, On the Revolution
of Heavenly Bodies. Siderius Nuncius, The Starry Messenger.
*He devoured each one, grateful that the schoolmaster had nailed
a spine of discipline into him. This was a wisdom as succulent as
his mother's songs, as rough as the lessons of his father.*

*From then on, the boy's eyes fixed on the knowledge before
him. His vision cooled. Where he once sprawled into fevered
dreams, his sight became sharp and honed. He saw theorems,
parabolas, calculations. Pythagoras's musical spheres. The tilted
axis of Copernicus. Hairline insights, etched into the frozen ice
of a page. He traced a filament, fine as a spider's web, from the
sun to Newton's retina. Its genius stunned him. He too could
dream with such precision.*

Fever

The summer I was twelve, the world seemed to open to me, as it once did for Newton, when he spread apart a light beam. To him, light was really the sum of separate strands of color, each made up of tiny particles.

That's how I often felt: I was the sum of all these new sensations running through me. Sometimes I believed I was filled with something hot and liquid and could pour myself into everything that surrounded me—the china-blue sky with its creamy dabs of clouds; my uncle's rose petals glistening with dew. Everything bent and melted. Everything was wet with promise.

Which is why the trouble began between my father and me.

Afternoons, I loved to sit on the garden wall at my aunt and uncle's and watch boys pass. They would whiz by on their bicycles, flash boastful grins and do hairpin turns. I found English boys ugly, with their weak chins and watery eyes. That didn't stop me from enjoying their attention, though. I would smile, put my hand on my hip, and shout back, "And what are *you* looking at?"

It felt good to sit on the wall, a cool breeze tickling my arms and back. My family didn't approve of the hours I spent there, yet their disapproval was part of my pleasure, as was the sensation of my bottom's hurting from the ledge. "Why you have to hang around the gate so much?" Aunt Inez asked me one day while she and my mother were setting up tea in the garden. Sheila had just arrived from Paris and was staying with us for a few weeks. Aunt Inez sat in a chair and heaved a sigh. "I don't know what will become of this girl. She's turning so wild."

My mother picked her way across the grass, teapot balanced in one hand, a tray of biscuits in the other. To my relief, she said, "Megan is her own person. Boys are a natural part of growing up."

"When I see Megan," Aunt Inez remarked, "it's like seeing my sister Didi all over again. We got to be careful."

"Why?" I noticed a sad cast to their eyes.

"Hush," my mother said. "It's just those old stories again. And don't talk like that, Inez. You'll scare the poor girl!"

"What happened to Didi?" I grabbed a biscuit.

Seeing my mother and my aunt exchange looks, I grinned and wiped the crumbs from my mouth. Whenever I heard their old tales, I liked to imagine myself flying over the red rooftops of Sudbury, to other places, chunks of stories I momentarily perched on.

"All right, Meggie," my aunt said. "I'll tell you, if you promise to stop hanging by the gate there. The neighbors will talk. And your father, you know how he is."

"I promise," I answered quickly, even though I knew I didn't mean it. I curled on the grass next to my aunt, my head resting on her thigh. Her voice rumbled through her warm skin as she talked.

"Your auntie Didi was so beautiful, Meggie, all she have to do is pin a flower to her hair and every village boy turn his head. Maywa's cousin, that Sonny boy, he was lovesick over your aunt. He used to stand outside the gate and sing." Aunt Inez's laughs were hearty and affectionate as she stroked my head.

"But your grandfather didn't want to let any of us out of his sight. Even if we were Presbyterian, we were also high Brahmin caste. No man could touch his daughters' skin unless the right blood ran through his veins."

"That's mean," I said, sitting up, but I remembered how, the other day, when my father set off to give his Thursday lecture at the library, his eyes narrowed at the sight of me. He was embarrassed, I sensed, by my milky-tea skin, the way my halter top barely grazed my waistband.

"The problem was, this was British Guiana, not India," my aunt explained. "And most of the good families move on to Georgetown or overseas. We have our high ways, but our house was fallin' down. My sisters turn bitter, seeing their youth slip from them. Poor Didi especially have a hard time of it. She couldn't keep her mind on her sewing or cooking. One day she set down her embroidery, walked through the yard and, as they say in the village, she gone wandering. No one knew where Didi went until a neighbor saw her walking by the back dam, singing one of Sonny's songs."

I imagined Aunt Didi drifting along the back dam as she listened for her singer, his song a far-off wind that stirred in her hair. Then I noticed a funny expression cross Aunt Inez's face as she went on.

"They bring her home, and the next day she slip away again. They find her hours later feeding a little goat by the schoolhouse. Once more she wander far and wide. This time, the minister bring her back by automobile a good day later. Her feet were all blistered, her hair fallen loose."

"Where did she go?" I asked.

Aunt Inez shook her head. "We don't know. But my mother get so upset she pay a visit to the obeah woman, who tell her that each time Didi get that look in her eyes, my mother got to bury an egg under the house steps. She bury an egg for each wistful move Didi make. If Didi stand on the verandah looking with sad eyes at the coconut palm, my mother done bury her egg. At first Didi keep wandering. Each time my mother bury another egg under a different step, Didi's circle get smaller, until soon she keeps circling her own home."

A soft, muddled look came into my aunt's eyes, as if she was being dragged from an old memory. She didn't notice my mother refill her teacup and press a napkin into her palm.

"Everyone in the village like to say our house catch the jumbee spirit." Aunt Inez absently put down her tea. "Every one of those eggs under the earth is like a dream unfulfilled. Each one hatched into a half-born bird-ghost. When the high wind blows, the bird-ghosts push through the dirt, their bad wings knock down branches. They rise and rise, let out their fury on those of us who dare run away and live out our dreams."

Aunt Inez's plump arms were tight against her chest, braced against something I couldn't see. I thought of my father, circling around his bedroom each night, a shudder in the window casements as the bird-ghosts swooped inside.

"That's why your father and I, it's like we catch some of that spirit. Sometimes I get so sad, it's all I can do to get out of my bed and not spend the whole day crying. Thank God for your uncle here who gives me a good shake and pushes me on. And your father, he's another one. That man kills himself with his work, running fast and hard so the spirit don't catch up with him."

We stared uncomfortably at one another. My aunt was hunched in the canvas seat, her face pulled into a wistful frown. She seemed far away from us.

My mother let out a peal of laughter. "Now Meggie, aren't you glad we raised you away from those old stories. You're beautiful and nobody is casting a spell on you."

I looked around the garden and at its reassuring sights— the teapot set on the grass, my uncle's shirts pinned to the clothesline. No matter what my mother said, I was sure something terrible could still happen to us. The bird-ghosts could come out in other ways, in the letters that nested in our mailboxes, the thin airmail kind with a stamp of Kaieteur Falls. Apparently, things had gotten very bad down there. A crazy man who liked purple-stitched saddles and voodoo ran the government. Men showed up at people's houses in the middle of the night, snatched away margarine tins, punished people if they found they'd bought a sack of flour on the black market. I couldn't tell if this was the craziness of Guyana or of my family, since it all seemed the same. I knew only that these letters kept coming and my poor uncle and aunts were stuck in our big family house, hungry, not even able to put marmalade on their toast.

There was trouble also here in the house in Sudbury, behind the walls, rustling in the corners. We were a house of people not getting what they wanted. Not my uncle, who trimmed his roses and tended his tomato plants, rattling the dustbins with a fury that scared me. And certainly not my mother, who spent her afternoons crocheting in the garden, twisting her sadness into squares of wool.

And not my cousin, whom I steadfastly avoided. When I first arrived in England this summer, George begged me to play a game made up from a TV show. I refused. How simple-minded he had become, I thought, his face soft and puppyish. Bit by bit our old friendship fell away, the little threads tearing at my heart. "You're not funny anymore," he finally complained. "I never was funny," I replied. "You just laughed at all the wrong things."

Yet the person who was having the most trouble was my father. Our night walks in the woods had grown longer. We sometimes traipsed miles, brambles stuck to our trouser legs, leaves clinging to our hair. One night he gripped my arm and told me, "You have a wonderful mind, with all I've taught you, Meggie. But you must be careful with your questions. The wrong ones can take you to terrible places. You can burn up with bad thoughts."

After that, I was sure I was to blame for my father's difficult summer. Every time I sat on the garden wall, I felt him at my back, pulling my steps in. It wasn't eggs he was planting; it was blue notecards filled with his tight, anxious scribbles, all about Newton's experiments, how he spread light into strands of violet and red bits. Newton was wrong too. *Squint harder,* my father wrote. *Don't believe what you see. You must see beyond, a beam of sunlight melts into a substratum of specks, melts again into honey-colored waves.*

Flip-flap, the cards went as he set them down on the desk. Every night I heard his heavy, sleepless tread as he circled around and around. *Our senses trick us. Reality is a vapor that drifts before our eyes. We are trapped in bodies that can't help us find the truth. Don't trust what you feel with that skin of yours. Don't stray too far. Don't leave me.* He was planting his cards outside my bedroom door, trying to draw the circuit of my thoughts tighter, to him.

The morning after I heard the story of the bird-ghosts, the gate clanged outside the house, and my aunt, my mother, and Sheila crowded at the bay window to see a woman march toward our door. A cream cloche topped her head, elegant as a perfect meringue. She wore a dress of iridescent blue-green material and walked briskly up the path.

"I can't believe it," Inez said, her tone both miffed and pleased as the woman reached the front stoop.

"Who is she?" my mother asked.

My aunt's voice lowered. "That's Mrs. Whyte. She's an American lady, married to an important cardiologist. You remember, she's the one your friend Arun called up last year, and who set up Warren's Thursday talks this summer at the Barham library."

Aunt Inez moved around the room, plumping pillows, shoving her frayed slippers under the sofa. When the doorbell rang, she patted her housedress and cast a glance at the door.

"La-di-dah," Sheila trilled, and sauntered into the hall. "The queen is coming to visit!"

"Stop it, Sheila, please." Aunt Inez pushed past Sheila with her broad shoulders, then swung open the door. "How do you do," she said in her most polite British voice.

It was amazing. With the tiniest brittle smile, Mrs. Whyte released a flood of brilliance into the hall that exposed us like frightened animals hidden behind Aunt Inez's sensible bulk. "Hello," she replied, her lips the same smooth, burnished pink-brown color as her curls. We watched, waiting, until she let out what sounded like a small burp, really a sweet hiccup of a laugh.

"The other day I was at Professor Singh's lecture, and I remembered his darling daughter from last summer. Then I was passing by yesterday and I saw her sitting on the wall, and I thought, Wouldn't it be splendid if she could meet my Peter! I believe they're about the same age. Peter is such a remarkable boy, and the two might hit it off." She drew in her breath and I did the same, dazzled that such a complicated story could be told about me.

"I understand Professor Singh is a bit strict with his daughter. That's so charming and old-world. So I thought I'd invite you to tea and he could see it's quite fine."

My face grew warm as all eyes turned to me, and Sheila and my mother made a little aisle. This seemed almost incredible, the world outside the garden softening to my every wish.

"Would you like to come play with my son?" Mrs. Whyte asked.

Even though I was thrilled, I wasn't sure what to make of this woman. Something in her manner made me mistrust her. I felt I was being used, but I could not guess what for. Her gaze roved to the cardboard boxes and suitcases that were propped under the coat rack. Every summer, with both families squeezed into the small house, belongings were kept in funny places. George's school clothes were stuffed into my parents' bulging suitcases in the corridor; potatoes sprouted out of a sewing basket next to extra bottles of orange squash. Now, under Mrs. Whyte's icy, appraising gaze, the house felt odd and cramped.

I nodded, my stomach twisted in a knot. "You must all come to tea, then," Mrs. Whyte said, and after chatting a few minutes more, she left.

After the door shut, Sheila winked. "Fancy lady seem to take a liking to Meggie."

"It's Warren she's taken a liking to," my mother said. "You know how it is. They all have crushes on him."

Sheila made a mocking face. "Oh, yeah. He do his little Caribbean-boy song-and-dance and they just suck it up!" She shook her head. "Some people never learn."

I was elated. It was me Mrs. Whyte had come to see! I walked around the house, an honored guest who deigned to visit her family. Nothing was good enough for me—not my aunt's cheese sandwiches with the crusts trimmed off, or George's offer to share his new watercolor set. I knew he was jealous, which delighted me even more.

"Stop your strutting, young lady," my aunt reprimanded.

"After all, George is in the same school as Peter and his sister Marge Whyte. Why didn't they visit before?"

"Because that woman's got wanderin' eyes." Sheila pointed upstairs, where my father was working.

Sitting in the Whytes' parlor, I felt as if we were strapped inside a rocket careening into a dangerous space warp. The bay window was a bubble of glass, the floors were polished blond wood, and the low furniture was made of bent metal and molded plastic. George and I shared a lounge strung with bristly ropes. Still in his lab coat, Dr. Whyte remained standing against a sleek black mantel as he sipped his tea.

Conversation teetered on a nervous blade. Aunt Inez must have felt rough and unkempt sitting on the smooth chairs. Mrs. Whyte fluttered about in a lime-green print dress that drifted around her bare arms and calves, a matching turban wrapped tight around her head. She gushed about how interesting my father's background was, how his parents had come from India and Ghana—no, Guinea—then she grew confused because Guinea wasn't in the Caribbean, was it?

"My dear, I believe you mean Guyana," Dr. Whyte corrected. "And up until a few years ago, Guyana was *British Guiana*, with an *i*."

I couldn't help feeling that it annoyed Dr. Whyte that the people in Guyana had switched the letter, like children left alone with a chalkboard who couldn't spell and mixed everything into a cloudy muddle. "We've got quite a few Guyanese people working at the clinic," he went on. For an instant, I panicked, wondering, Could Maywa have done all those strange things at Dr. Whyte's clinic?

"A lot of people are coming over here," my aunt said. She was getting heated up, as always happened when talk turned to other Guyanese and the situation in the country. "The politics so bad over there. They making the people bad too," she added with a sniff, then winced when she realized that her British accent had lapsed.

For a few minutes the grown-ups sipped their tea and ate their biscuits, while I stole looks at Peter Whyte.

"I understand your lectures have become quite popular," ventured Dr. Whyte.

"That's right." My father mashed a handkerchief against his neck. His brow was a glossy brown. I had never seen him sweat so much. I wanted to rush across the room, cover him up.

"I was thinking that maybe we would help Professor Singh," Mrs. Whyte said. "He's hoping to present his findings at Cambridge." When her husband didn't respond, she pressed on. "Professor Singh talks in that sweet accent and tells all these lovely stories, you hardly know it's philosophy he's talking about."

My aunt and mother pursed their lips, but their smiles still showed through. My father crossed and recrossed his feet. I knew what he was thinking. He was ashamed of the way Mrs. Whyte talked about him. People sometimes called my father the ca- lypso lecturer at his college, and he didn't like it very much. "I'm a serious professor," he used to complain to my mother. "I'm not a singer on a cruise ship."

Mrs. Whyte pinched the frilly edge of her collar and shook

it to cool herself off. "Go on. Tell them the story about how when you were a little boy you had your own vision of light."

I could hear Dr. Whyte's cup scrape against his saucer as he waited for my father to step forward and flourish his exotic colors. It was then that I understood what scared me about Mrs. Whyte's eyes. Sheila was right. They did wander. They flew about, picked up bits of what they hungered for. They especially seized on my father and scavenged every detail of him—his hands knotted in his lap, black, curly hair that glistened with Brylcreem as he stared glumly at his toes. I couldn't understand why the thin man at the mantel frightened him.

"Go on," Mrs. Whyte urged.

"Yes, yes!" my father said, too loud. But he seemed unable to find the words to describe his vision. After a few beats, Dr. Whyte glanced at his watch and said, "You'll have to excuse me. I must see to a patient over at the clinic."

"Of course!" my father bellowed, and stood. "I have work to do too."

Everyone stood. Teacups rattled, hands were thrust out, my aunt touched her hair, and my mother looked relieved and exhausted. Mrs. Whyte directed me and the other four children out the rear door.

Before stepping outside, I heard a scuffling in the hall. I saw Mrs. Whyte grasp my father by the arm and lean close.

"Don't worry," I heard her assure him. "You can tell your story another day." One of her laughs popped gently into the air. This time, I realized it was Mrs. Whyte's hand that was doing the wandering. It crept under the flap of my father's suit jacket and made a quick, circular motion on his back. My father went rigid, and a slow shudder worked its way from the tips of his shoes, through his chest, to his sweaty, anguished face.

While the adults scattered, we kids flew into the garden. Now I could get a good look at this new boy Peter Whyte. His face reminded me of a bowl of soft custard; his stomach eased into thick legs. I wanted to poke my fingers into his knees and make two perfect dimples.

I could feel Peter's eyes raking me up and down, and I liked it, for I found him peculiar and challenging. First he gave me a geography test and demanded to know where Guyana was, which I dutifully informed him was in northern South America and looked like a little flat cracker you could break off. Next he ran through the monarchs of England, which impressed and bored me. I gave him a rundown of my favorite Mets from the 1969 World Series.

"Since my dad's a doctor," he declared, "that's what I'm going to be when I grow up. What about you?"

"I'm going to help my father," I replied. "He's a philosopher."

"That right? Do you believe in God?"

I nodded.

"I don't," he told me. "When a person dies, the body rots to nothing."

I felt an itchy warmth on my skin. Peter made me curious, jittery with weird thoughts. I imagined a skull lying on the grass behind him, its brain shriveled to a dried pea.

"Tell me what your father has taught you," he said.

"Okay." I explained that the chapter my father was now writing was about how our eyes were no good because we couldn't really see what light was.

Peter shook his head. "That's stupid. Scientists have sent people to the moon, and they found a vaccine for polio, so surely they can figure out something about a dumb light that comes from a bulb."

"Oh, yeah?" I said. "It's not so easy, it's been stumping them for a zillion years." Peter's round, indignant face quieted me, and a fog confusion rose in my mind.

"Peter!" We both turned to see Marge a few feet away, hands on hips, an exasperated look on her face. "What about *us*?"

I had already sized Marge up as dopey, better for George anyway. With her cascade of toffee-brown curls, she looked like an ice cream sundae, piled too high. Each time she tittered, she covered her mouth with a plump hand and collapsed into a sweet, sticky mush.

Peter crossed his arms on his chest, thought for a moment, and told us that we were going to play surgery. George and Marge dropped down obediently on the grass while Peter and I went to get a box of Dr. Whyte's discarded supplies. For the next hour we swabbed their imaginary wounds with bandages and sour-smelling concoctions made of berries and detergent.

Eventually Peter and I tired of this game. He poked me in the ribs and said, "Listen here, I have a laboratory in my basement and I'm going to fetch some things for it. You want to come along?"

I followed him excitedly out of the garden and down the street. Together we explored the nearby alleyways and rummaged through the butcher's trash bins, where Peter pulled out the slick ropes of a pig's intestines and a cleaned shoulder bone. Behind the grocer's and the pharmacy we found three brown eggs, a cracked jar of Vaseline, and a mousetrap. We returned to Peter's house and, crouched in the basement, sorted our findings in shoe boxes. The air was spiced with dust, the oil burner breathed near. I knew I shouldn't stay down there too long, especially when I felt Peter's sweaty fingers stray to the bottom of my spine.

Every day for the next two weeks, he and I played in his basement, where brown shadows fell on greasy newspaper and a white-hot sky beat through the window screen. We sliced open dried insects with his penknife, tweaked off their wispy antennae. I could not get enough of my new friend. What the Whytes built up in propriety Peter struck down with his fiendish curiosity—a curiosity that seemed perfectly matched to my own. I began to need Peter desperately, with his fierce and unusual sense of the world.

Then we discovered the closet, the one in his parents' bedroom. I liked to kneel in the narrow space, pungent with cedar, and where Mrs. Whyte's Popsicle-colored clothes hung heavy above my head. They were like warm animals, fur combed to a silky finish, arms dangling. I loved the smooth cuffs that brushed my cheek, loved to feel my knees tipped against the toes of Mrs. Whyte's racked high heels. I would mash my face into her herringbone skirts, rub the angora dress until it spit out electric sparks. Sometimes I balanced a pump toward me and drank in its musty perfume of sweat and leather insoles worn papersmooth. A strange thrill coursed through me; goose bumps pricked my arms.

Here Peter and I played our game. I would wait in the closet until I heard the click of a latch and brightness from the plastic globe spilled across the floor. Then we were surrounded by dark again, knees touching. In the thick forest of polyesters and Shetland wools, Peter draped an object on the tender inside of my arm—a banana peel, a wet, bloated tea bag—and I tried to guess what it was.

It was an awful game and I loved it. I never knew what Peter had brought and, of course, always suspected the worst. The dark seethed, took on its own uncanny shapes, and pulsed with horrid creatures—earthworms, dead termites, lopped-off mouse tails. We drove ourselves into a gasping, fearful heat until I could bear it no longer. I would throw myself against the door and tumble outside to brush off a harmless potato slice.

After our laughter had subsided, Peter often rolled next to me on the carpet. "Your family's swell," he would say. "Why can't we play at your house?"

"I don't think that's a good idea," I would reply, and turn my face away.

Even with our games, Peter's house was empty and clear. I could hear myself think there. I knew no one bumped overhead or swooped down to tell me crazy tales; no mother lingered in doorways, no father muttered; no jabbery creatures hid in the closets.

I didn't want to come from such a sad family, always yearning and jealous. I wanted to get what I aimed for, just like Mrs. Whyte with her horsey mouth, and live in a house like this, with blond wood floors and chairs of bent metal and closets that smelled of cedar, no letters from Guyana sliding through the mail slot with a scary hiss; no funny people calling to ask for money; no stories that jumbled me up so I didn't know who I was.

Since our tea with the Whytes, my father seemed to shrink further into himself. One Thursday he canceled his lecture because he had a cold; he sat in a sunny spot in the garden, bundled under one of my mother's afghans. He felt well enough, though, to accept a visit from Mrs. Whyte, who brought him a pouch of his favorite tobacco. Despite myself, and despite the suspicious looks my mother and aunt sent through the curtains, I admired Mrs. Whyte. She walked across the grass, cut the air with her big elbows and long legs, and placed her chair close to his, so she could lavish her goofy praise on him.

After this visit my father grew even more harsh with me. "Off with that boy again?" he asked me each time I was about to leave the house. "I don't like this," he told my mother. "I didn't raise my daughter to go gallivanting around."

At this, my mother's eyes flowed with tears. "It doesn't stop you from gallivanting off with that Mrs. Whyte," she retorted.

"This is different. Mrs. Whyte is helping me with some connections."

Mrs. Whyte really did appear to be working on some connections. I heard of phone calls, mysterious meetings at the Whytes' house. But the effect on my father was strange. Soon he took to uttering proclamations about the Whytes. "There's danger in that house," he warned me. "Those people appear to be one thing, Meggie, but are another. That house is really a place of darkness and flesh. Be careful."

I was sprinting down the stairs one day when I heard his sharp rasp at my back. "Where are you off to, young lady?" He stood in the bedroom doorway, red silk robe tied at an angle, revealing old pajama pants. It was almost noon.

He gestured toward the bedroom, which doubled as his study during the day. The air was stale with pipe smoke, balled-up notes littered the desk, teacups lined the windowsill. When I saw the mussed sheets, a hot flush crept over my cheeks. His fingers latched around my wrist and I was pulled inside. Under the thin robe, his skin reeked of sweat, which made me queasy.

"Yesterday I looked for you, but you were off somewhere. Where were you?"

"At Peter's," I answered.

"Where?"

"Peter's."

"And what of me?"

I tried to press down the urge to dart outside. "I'm sorry," I said, as much to get away from his damp smell and sad eyes as anything else.

He seized a book from his desk. " 'For light doth seize my brain,' " he read, " 'with frantic pain.' "

Placing the book down, he turned to me. "Do you know what that means, Meggie? Do you know the sacrifices I put up with? I don't go out! I don't do anything! I stay here, day after day. Do you have any idea what is dragging at me? Is it so much to ask my daughter to spare a few moments for her father?"

"No." My voice was weak, drowning sound, sucked into a watery hole.

"If you could just stay put. Just. Stay. Put."

He grabbed his blue notecards, loosened the rubber bands, and slapped the cards in a ragged circle on the floor, from the wardrobe to the desk to the doorjamb. Then he gave a fierce

kick. Several cards spun toward the desk. I watched anxiously as he kicked again and a few cards skittered under the bed. I shivered. The window sash banged. My father muttered under his breath about flesh again, and I could hear the soft flap of bird-ghosts gathering on the sill. More and more cards, until I was dizzy from the whir of blue. There was a faint rustle of feathers. The room shut. The quiet and the dark were suffocating.

My father cinched his fingers around my wrist, and shook it roughly. "You see what you've done to me, all the time playing with that boy!"

A new scorn struggled to my lips. "You like Mrs. Whyte all right," I blurted out.

His face flattened in surprise, and a slow fury trembled across his cheeks. "I don't know what's happened to you," he said. "You used to be my daughter. Now you're just a girl with a fresh mouth."

I ran the whole way to Peter's, let myself in through the rear door, and padded upstairs to his parents' closet, where I shut the door behind me and leaned against a suitcase. There I balanced on my haunches, rocked back and forth in a soothing rhythm, protected by the perfumed shapes of Mrs. Whyte's clothes. Blood pounded loudly in my temples; it sounded like ant-sized men marching in the whorls of my ears. I was safe here, I thought. Safe from my father and his ugly words.

For the first time I looked closely at darkness and saw it was really shadow webbed with fine, bright cracks. I saw sparks of silver-white, like flecks of calcite in rock. Were these Newton's light particles, I wondered, these dancing points that pricked my eyes? Doubt the senses, my father had taught me. What was I made of? The body, or strength of mind? I stared until specks gathered into knots, sprang loose again. The spots drew into shapes, and I realized they were bodies moving outside.

I eased the door open a sliver to see my father sitting on the bed. He was dressed now, though still disheveled, shirt jammed into his pants, hair uncombed. My breaths quickened; I feared he had come to punish me. Then I heard another voice and realized my father was next to Mrs. Whyte. I rubbed my eyes, not sure what I was seeing.

They sat side by side, doing nothing until Mrs. Whyte took my father's hand into her lap and began to stroke the inside of his arm. A strange expression flared across his face—first excitement, then revulsion, then excitement again. "You're of another world," Mrs. Whyte said, as her hand moved to my father's shoulder. "That's what I like about you, Warren."

At the sound of his name, my father's shoulders twitched; I too felt a jolt, and nearly fell over on my knees. By the time I had righted myself, Mrs. Whyte had put her arms around my father's neck and was talking softly into his hair. I could not stop watching, but an angry burn crawled from my stomach to my mouth. Don't touch him, I thought, don't you dare touch him.

Not only was Mrs. Whyte touching my father, she had unbuttoned her blouse and was wriggling free of the sleeves. The sight of Mrs. Whyte, the sag of her lace bra cups, her wide sloping hips, alarmed me. I could see it alarmed my father too; he got up from the bed and hurried toward the closet.

For an instant, as the door opened, I was caught under the lamp's glare, sure my father could see me. His hands ran across the clothes until he found a red-striped blouse and took it off the hanger. The door swung half shut and I saw that he was arranging the blouse around her bare shoulders. "You are so silly!" she exclaimed, and the two of them fell and tussled on the bed. It was a game. He lunged and covered her with the blouse, she snaked it off her shoulders and planted small kisses on his cheek.

He returned to the closet and chose a lemon-colored knit top, which he tried to smooth down over her head. When his hands reached her breasts, he paused. "You see," she said, smiling. They were at it again, rolling and tackling each other on the bedspread, until my father broke free to grab another article of clothing.

They were in a rhythm, and I was part of the rhythm too. Each time the plastic globe flashed like a moon on my terrified face, each time it clicked shut and left me in a swampy, guilty darkness, I knew my father and I were joined in a fright that bathed us both in a raw sweat. His skin glowed with heat and shame. Sweat pooled in the back of my knees. I was sure he didn't really want to be with Mrs. Whyte. Just as when I played with Peter, this was part of the game, the sweet torture where your will and your body twisted, split, and fused again.

Once more my father reached into the folds of the closet. He froze at a new noise. Peter's voice floated into the room. "Hullo?" he called. "Anyone here?"

"Oh, no," I heard Mrs. Whyte cry.

"No!" I yelled, shoved against the door, and fell out. Clothes slid to the floor, Mrs. Whyte's russet hair made two static wings. She covered her face with her hands and moaned, "This is terrible."

As I streaked past her, I saw a dark nipple pressed against the lace bra cup. My father was stuck in the middle of the room; a suede patchwork vest dropped to the floor. I felt Peter drag me from the room, down the stairs, and outside.

For a few minutes there were only the sounds of our feet on earth, the snap of branches, Peter gulping air down. My own breaths hurt, tears salted my cheeks.

Peter waded through a thicket of bushes and dropped down by a stream bed. From between two rocks, he fished out an olive-green frog, legs held between his thumb and forefinger. "Bet you a shilling I can swallow this whole," he said. His jaw had tensed into a hard expression I had never seen before.

"Peter, are you okay?" I asked.

"Shut up."

The frog's belly twitched. It gave a few heavy-lidded blinks as Peter tilted his head back and dropped the squirming creature into his mouth. His cheeks puffed out, brownish-green ooze slid down his chin.

A bubble of nausea popped in me. Watching his Adam's apple move up and down, I was fascinated too. He had succeeded in swallowing the terrible sight of my father and Mrs. Whyte in the bedroom. Peter scooped water from the stream into his palms and noisily drank. When he raised his face to me, his eyes were bright with triumph; he knew he had done something wonderfully cruel. Now I had no choice but to follow him farther into the woods.

We began another game, in which Peter plucked at things

and tested me. "Smell," he ordered. He crushed a leaf under my nose, and a sweet odor drifted up. "I won't tell you what it is," he informed me. "You must learn it by its smell, not its name."

We reached the clearing where I often walked with my father. Sunshine covered the ground in mustard-colored spots. "Lie down," he demanded. I obeyed. I felt I was watching myself from the curving trees, seeing Peter with another girl, her movements wooden and confused.

He brushed leaves on my face. They felt lovely and cool, and I tilted my chin up like a kitten. Tickles gathered in the hollow of my neck, a faint burn that burst into heat near my navel. I was dropping into my skin, each new sensation lapping in circles as he moved farther down, to my waist. He made me do the same to him, brushing the leaf tips on his belly.

Overhead, a bird chirped, like a baby gasping for breath.

"Peter," I asked, "what kind of bird is that?"

"Shut up." He grabbed my arm. "Don't you ever wonder what the body is made of? What skin and bones and muscles *really* are?"

The bird let out a raw-throated song. Something itched behind my eyes. "Peter, let's go back." I added softly, "Please."

"No. We're not done. First you have to rub these leaves under your shirt. I want to see if your skin reacts the same all over."

I did exactly as he said. I stroked my chest, around the buds of my nipples. I was that other girl under the watchful trees who did not know her own will from that of the boy who loomed over her. A dirty feeling gathered in the pit of my stomach as I fought back tears.

When I saw he wasn't looking anymore, I tossed the leaves

away and watched them flutter like triangles of burning paper on the ground. We got to our feet and began to run, hard. In less than an hour, I had lost a clear vision of myself, and I watched it sink from my mind.

"Don't you know poison oak when you see it?" my aunt asked.

When I lifted my face from the pillow, I saw Aunt Inez, Uncle Tom, and my parents at the foot of my bed, their faces creased with worry. I tried to answer, but my lips cracked with fire. Dry patches crumbled on my cheeks.

"Hush, Inez," my mother said. She stepped closer and palmed something slick and wet—calamine lotion—on my chest and arms. "They didn't know any better. They were just curious. There's no harm in a child's curiosity."

"Curiosity, my foot!" my father charged. "I know what was really going on."

Another face pushed through. Peter! Only his head was stretched from top to bottom. Stern blue eyes showed behind his glasses. This wasn't Peter but a grown-up version, Dr. Whyte. A black snake was attached to his chin and divided into two tails that disappeared into each ear. Its cold mouth probed my ribs. A stethoscope, just like the one Peter kept in his laboratory.

"She has a fever," Dr. Whyte explained.

"Fever is bad," my father asserted. "Meggie is the same as me. All the demons come out, like bad luck."

"Enough of that old village talk," my mother said. "You'll scare her."

Dr. Whyte droned on about how leaves secrete a sap, which

irritates the skin and causes a rise in body temperature. I hated listening to him. Each sentence was a corridor of cold white rooms that opened into more empty rooms. I twisted in the sheets, and my thoughts became ticklish. Daddy, I wanted to call out, did you know air was really a sponge? Do you know where light goes when lamps are turned off? It's seeped into the air, specks of light-dust winking at me from their secret holes!

My family was gone. Only my father remained. He sat on the edge of my bed, his head in his hands. "It's all my fault," he said. "I push you too hard. Always in one direction. Why, always why, I keep telling you to ask." He sighed. "I make you un-happy."

"I'm not unhappy."

My father patted my head. "Maybe not now," he said. "Things come out later."

The walls buckled into place. Questions formed, each an oval of sound that dissolved into the next. "Why, always why." Mrs. Whyte's lace bra cups. Peter and me in the woods, tipping rocks over. Thick fingers, touching me.

Something wet was swabbed on my stomach. It reminded me of Peter's brushing leaves over my skin. What could turn a delightful feeling into poison, so the body burned? How about the bird cawing in the tree? The ground broke open, the air was too hot. A chilled wad on my forehead. "Just relax," they told me. The bird! I can see it hover above us, its trembling throat, its heart beating a hundred times a minute. I heard it now. The bird sang.

"Meggie, stop talking and lie still." A tablet was slipped be-tween my cracked lips. The singing stopped.

———

Sometime in the middle of the night the bird-ghosts were released. They flew into my room and hopped around the circle of ashes my fever had burned. You got to eat, they cackled. You got to be good so you can grow up to be special, like your father wants. Wing bones covered my face. I beat them back. One tore a strip of flesh from my ribs.

Stop! I screamed. With a click, the room was filled with yellow air. The birds shrank into the bureau drawers. Someone lifted me, a strong arm against my back. I was being carried down the stairs. Who was holding me? A door opened and we passed through, to the garden. Around us lay a starless night, the sweet odor of roses.

This was my father. He kept me close, his voice full of sadness. "There, there, Meggie," he said. "I know how it is. They come out, in the dark. We know how to take care of them."

His knees cracked as he propped me across his lap. I am too big, too old to be carried like this, I thought as he paused to catch his breath. He was rubbing cold dirt on my heels.

"My mother did this to me, when I wandered too far," he told me. "She say, 'Warren, you see bad things because your feet are no longer planted on this earth. Your feet stop walking on the ground and travel in the air, to spirits and bad visions.' "

"What about Peter?" I asked. "Why did he hurt me on purpose?"

"I warned you." My father's nails scratched my arms. "You got to be careful about who you let touch your beautiful skin. I made a mistake too, Meggie. We can't let the wrong people touch us. Otherwise their fire will eat up all our questions."

I curled tighter, ashamed of what I had done, ashamed for the both of us.

His fingers ground dirt between my toes. He gave each of my soles a firm smack and stood again.

"You can put me down now," I said, surprised at my own clearness.

"No, no. You're not ready. You must wait. Otherwise it doesn't work."

He pulled a white bone from his pocket and scraped a small rut in the ground with his fingers. The bone twirled from his hand and he covered the hole. "Fever!" he shouted. "Be gone with the bone!" He sang a song whose words I didn't know.

The hedges parted and a figure walked toward us, dry leaves dropping from her mouth. I knew it was Aunt Didi. Is that what happens when the bird-ghosts come for you? I wanted to ask her as she kneeled before me and draped a garland of flowers around my shoulders. The flowers, I saw, were made of bones.

"Leave me alone!" I cried.

My father held me again. The earth was cool on my feet. My father kissed them, his lips dry and moist as they inched along my soles.

More dirt slapped between my toes, a jumble of words. And even though the phrases made no sense, they slowly took shape in my mind. A sense of something age-old. I'm sorry, his grip seemed to say. I'm so sorry.

We stayed in the garden a long time.

I was not well for many weeks. The fever burned a tiny white star in my head that left me dazed and weak. It was only when I was near my father that I felt safe and could hear my own thoughts. I walked around the garden, and easily grew tired. The bright summer sky, the cars rushing past on the other side of the wall could exhaust me. Once I tried to go to the ice cream shop and began to shake the moment I put one foot outside the gate. I understood better why Aunt Didi had come back home. *Flip-flap*, the cards went, pulling your steps in. It felt good, knowing where I belonged, our secret floating like a small, glowing egg between my father and me.

All summer I continued not to be myself. Or maybe I never did become myself. I was watching that girl from the eaves, spying on her from between the hedges. Sometimes I heard voices say nasty things about me. Or I cried for no reason at all. Lying in bed, I grew convinced that the trees outside would bend forward, shatter the window, and release something black and awful.

One night while I was standing by the gate, a shout rang out. A group of boys had gathered on the corner. There might have been four or five of them, but in the dark, they looked like a single creature with too many heads and extra legs. One boy separated himself and called to me. "Meggie, you want to join us?" When I saw the rounds of his spectacles, the plump knees, my heart jumped. It was Peter.

I hesitated, an answer warming my lips. I longed to run up to him and playfully punch his arm. Then I grew ashamed and was pulled down inside myself. "Too good for us?" another boy shouted as I turned my back and started up the path. "Go on, stay home!"

I hardly heard them, hardly cared. They could not know how superior I felt as I headed into the house, where a man sat bent over a book, in a circle of brightness only I could step inside. They could not know the scene that had scored itself on my skin; how I could always return to that night in the garden, when I was surrounded by the immensity and darkness of my father's love.

Year after year, the boy walked in his family's cane fields,
dreaming of his good future, of the secret fire he would one day
forge into speech. He burned with ambition. He could not wait
for the day he would set off across the ocean, go to school and
find the answers to his questions.

He read all the time—early in the morning, when the
workers headed down the road, grass blades strapped to their
backs, and late at night, under the kerosene lamp, until the print
turned runny and soft under his eyes. All the girls wanted to
marry this boy, with his floppy black hair, his love of figures and
talk. He studied everything—history, philosophy—his mind lit
with ideas, leaping through hoops of reason. He especially loved
the dry, mathematical dots of physics.

The Professor of Light

Nights, he dreamed of Michael Faraday, the blacksmith's son, who tied two wires to a magnet, and blasted open a new world bristling with electromagnetic waves. He saw the flint blue of Faraday's workshop, heat and sparks. Coils, wires, soldering lead. In the humming song of electrons, did Faraday hear the shriek of iron on anvil? Did he see, in that simple act, the shadow of his father's hammer, falling?

Near the boiling house, the boy's own father watched his son's restless walks. He did not like what he saw. He burned with a different kind of passion. He believed all the answers lay in their little village, where he had planted his sugar cane. He dragged his son to the boiling house and taught him to make their rum strong. For every pot his father made, the boy learned to throw his anger and hard luck inside. Everyone said the father's rum glowed like a wild fire that scorched their heads. The pandits warned him, Beware, all children want to steal their parents' passion for their own destiny.

One night the boy sneaked inside the boiling house. "That old fool doing the wrong thing," he told himself, and filled a pot with the terrible rum. He balanced the pot on the edge of a boat, to illuminate the way to the answers he wanted. Suddenly his father came running to the water's edge, and let out a howl so loud that waves crashed against his boat. "You damn cursed boy!" he shouted. "How dare you take what's mine for your empty-head ideas!"

The boy was so frightened he pushed the boat from the shore and spilled all the rum. Desolate, he thought, I am lost! I'm never going to find anything! But the rum cooled to crystals that guided him through the dark. The last he saw of his father, he was standing on the shore with his empty pot, shaking his fist.

The boy kept going, searching for his answers in the crystals. But he was careful too. From that night on, he watched behind him, for he had stolen his own father's passion. After all, he never knew when that vengeful man might rise and steal it back.

The Cure

The summer I was thirteen I needed to step forward and save my father. And it was Uncle Tom who taught me the discipline to do so, how to stay quiet and save someone, with small things, in small ways.

By now I'd come to see that my father's search into light grew more intense in the summer because who we were—a funny, in-between family, Indian, Caribbean, American, English—was clearer during the months we spent in Sudbury. My father's book was both a wish to understand us and an inquiry into particle and wave. And why not? Weren't we particle and wave, the stream of old stories passing through?

Over the year my parents had been fighting, even more than in the old days. My mother kept complaining that she wanted a *real* vacation. "What do you mean, a real vacation?" my father often said. "You get to live in England, what's so bad about that?"

"Cooking and living in your sister's house isn't exactly a vacation," she would retort. "You can do better than that."

My mother had gained a lot of weight during the winter. It was strange to see her milky skin spread like a thick cream around her arms and hips, the small hump of her stomach, as if she was always waterlogged. Usually fashion-conscious, she even stooped to buying a purple polyester pantsuit from Sears. One day she went to the hairdresser's and had her hair dyed a horrible strawberry-copper; the ends frizzed like torn electrical wires. Though she moved slower because of the extra weight, a hot, miserable agitation sizzled in her veins.

My father, in contrast, seemed to shed his skin. Dry, ashy eczema spotted his nut-brown arms and legs. A rash grew on his calf; it resembled a torn piece of carbon paper, the edges a frayed blue. He went to doctors, who prescribed various ointments. Nothing worked. He kept scratching the rash, until it turned into a raging sore.

To make matters worse, letters from Guyana kept arriving. The news was dreadful—the house was falling apart, and Brother Joseph was worse. My father kept sending checks, but the money didn't reach them. It was stolen by some second cousin at the gas station to which the letters were sent, or maybe it was his nephew, no one was sure. Even Sheila, after her last trip, swore she would not return Guyana. It was very bad there, she said, people walked around with masks for faces, and in this country that once shimmered with green paddy fields, there was no rice.

After we arrived in Sudbury, a terrible nostalgia shook through the house. My father dragged around, talking about the brier tree, the ghosts. For a few days he sent me to the newsagent's for tobacco and pipe cleaners; he would shut the curtains and remain in the bedroom, where he kept up his fretful pacing. Aunt Inez wept behind closed doors. I could hear how hard it was for my uncle to wake her when he brought her tea in the morning.

A blue aerogram arrived, and it sat, unopened, on my father's bureau. Then another, this one ripped up without his having opened it. Soon there were packages, meant to work their persuasive charms: small pillows embroidered by Aunt Didi, slender prayerbooks from the Presbyterian church, guavas wrapped in pink tissue.

I imagined my aunts in the old family house, and my grandparents' ghosts banging at the shutters. I could see my aunt Edith swim toward us, her jewelry loosening from her ears and wrists; she lifted her skirt, climbed over the garden gate, walked up the path, rapped firmly at the door, and demanded her check. Uncle Joseph trailed behind her, cheeks smeared with mud. The Sudbury house seemed to fill with murky water. The downstairs rooms were soon flooded by a tide of soiled letters, all the letters my father had refused to answer, which swept upstairs to the bedroom, where he paced and wished the past would stop tugging at his ankles.

We were having tea one afternoon when we heard a high, perky beep outside and moments later Uncle Tom rushed in. He wore a light-gray jacket and a checked cap slanted over his eyes. "Hullo!" he greeted us. "Just thought I'd tell you. I've made reservations at a guesthouse in Brighton."

Reservations at what? we clamored. When? How would we get there?

"We'll drive," he replied.

"Nonsense," Aunt Inez said. "You don't even have a license yet."

At this, Uncle Tom folded his palms together, like a reverend about to give a blessing. "I've passed my test." Then he was leading us out the door, through the garden to the front curb, where a whey-colored Austin-Healey, crowned by a luggage rack, waited.

"Tom!" Aunt Inez gasped. "You didn't——"

"Rental," he reassured her. "Three weeks. We leave for Brighton in two days."

We were all stunned. Not only did we not know that Uncle Tom had scheduled—and passed—his driving test, but we did not believe that he could come up with such an elaborate plan, send for brochures, talk in secret to a guesthouse, spend money!

Before anyone could object, he went upstairs, knocked on my father's door, brought him outside, and told him he was coming for a drive. "I'm busy," my father said. He cast a suspicious glance at the luggage rack.

"All the more reason to hurry up. Come on, hop to it!"

To my amazement, my uncle hustled my father inside the car, along with us kids. We scooted across the smooth, factory-smelling seats.

My uncle drove terribly. He put his hands not at the ten-o'clock and two-o'clock positions—as even I knew you were supposed to—but at five and seven. He released the wheel like a slippery rope, and appeared unwilling to let go of the clutch. The wheel twitched, the car lurched, and in herky-jerky fashion we made it around the block and back to the house, where Aunt Inez and my mother stood at the gate waving.

"Enough," my father declared. He pulled his handkerchief from his pocket to mop his brow. Ignoring him, my uncle steered the car into traffic, and this time circled a four-block radius, passing the butcher's and the train station. My father fumed and sweated in the front seat.

"We need some time off, fresh air, walks on the beach," Uncle Tom was saying.

I was amazed at his force. He was always so quiet. Aunt Inez's crying jags must have scared him. The house *had* grown too gloomy. Maybe, I reflected, her crying fits reminded him of the year after they married and my aunt nearly rotted the house with her weeping. And he was scared too of the endless flood of letters.

As the car turned the corner yet another time, I understood this was my uncle's way of keeping us tight to his rein. Around and around we went, like my uncle's routines, wash one shirt every morning, water the plants every other day, rubbish on Thursday nights. Once more we circled the familiar Sudbury streets, my father cursing under his breath. Uncle Tom was determined to cure the family of its ills; he pulled us in through these small, determined gestures, so we wouldn't go wandering off.

The holiday was a good idea. My father was at an important crossroads in his book. Once Michael Faraday had switched on his magnetic coils, light was seen as fields of electromagnetic waves. Next came Einstein's discovery of light as little lumps of energy called photons. The universe of understanding would divide into particle and wave, the very fork that my father wanted to dive between. He wanted to peel back the membrane of words and calculations, and find his own truth where opposites did not exist.

To do my part, I had learned to type. I convinced the Specially Gifted Program counselor at my junior high that it made more sense to let me take vocational skills than art. For one period a day, I sat in a drab, high-ceilinged room, an old Remington bolted to each table, and swiftly moved from *The quick brown fox jumps over the lazy dog* to bona fide business letters. The class was filled with stupid girls with painted nails and feathered hairdos who would one day be secretaries. The teacher, Mrs. Coppin, actually boxed our ears if she caught us regressing to the two-finger hunt-and-peck method. She taught us headings, dates, four returns before the company's address, two for the salutation. I had a far greater mission than business letters. I was going to organize and type the next chapter of my father's book. By the end of the school year, I was a pretty swift forty-five words a minute—not bad, by my estimation.

Before we left for England, with my babysitting money and saved-up allowance, I bought a portable Smith-Corona boasting a teal-blue vinyl cover that I loved to flick off every morning, like Mary Tyler Moore in her newsroom. The keys were smooth as buttons, with perfect-sized hollows for my finger pads, and jumped back with an inspiring, jazzy bounce. Now not only did I sort my father's notes, but I organized and typed the scribbles from his blue notecards onto onionskin paper. As I typed in my

Sudbury bedroom, my father's thoughts surged through my
bones in hopeful currents. *Tap-tap,* I went, flying quick as the
electromagnetic waves my father wrote about. *Tap-tap,* light is
nothing more than electricity surging across the air. We would
finish the book this summer, I was sure of it.

Two days after Uncle Tom brought home the rental car, we
loaded the suitcases with shorts and towels, a Styrofoam kick-
board for Timmy, books for my father, a new bathing suit fes-
tooned with a white pleated skirt for my aunt, along with various
ointments for my father's skin, diet pills and cellulite-vanishing
oil for my mother, who had heard about marvelous saltwater
pools at Brighton and was determined to lose fifteen pounds in
the next few weeks.

It was late morning when we got into the car. We drove and
drove, the poor Austin-Healey heaving like an overburdened
camel, and reached Brighton in the afternoon. As we turned a
corner, I could feel everyone release a sigh of disappointment.

Before us were banks of flashing game arcades, saltwater
taffy and candy-apple stands, magenta-bulbed signs advertising
tarot readers, and a giant motorized statue with Aladdin-style
slippers, rumbling out a hollow laugh. An ugly, mangled beast of
an amusement park reared up, with too many curving limbs and
tails.

The beach was also disappointing. I had been thinking
American beach—radios fizzing, druggy smell of suntan oil,
glistening honeyed bodies. I could not believe that this stretch of
gray pebbles, with a weak sun in the overcast sky, could be called
a beach. I should have known. This was where Aunt Inez had

plunged her feet into the stones and decided to marry Uncle Tom.

My uncle inched the car down a narrow road that led to our guesthouse. It was a crooked white stucco house, with its own garden. Still, George and I jumped up in our seats when we saw the orange lilies, the trellis ornate with droopy roses. It looked like a fairy-tale garden, though already, as we pulled our luggage across the brick path, Uncle Tom was criticizing the lumpy flower beds planted too close to one another.

"Looks like you've got your work cut out for you," Aunt Inez told him.

Our guesthouse smelled damp—damp sheets, damp closets, the striped-wallpaper walls moist with a suspicious brown film. I was given my own room, with a dormer window, underneath which I wedged a narrow table and set up my typewriter. From there, I could view across the garden to the water and the octopus ride. Dabs of green and blue shimmied up and down the octopus's tentacles, the orbed seats spun brightly. I liked my view. The ride reminded me of an electron, shooting out spikes of bright energy.

"That's a stupid plan," George told me over breakfast when I informed him I intended to spend the morning typing up my father's most recent packet of notecards. I had decided to forgive George his slowness from the previous summer, since he looked so cute in his red drawstring bathing suit, a white towel slung coyly over his shoulder. George wasn't around much these days; he had a whole new set of friends—*girl*friends, my aunt liked to say with a smirk.

"What's so stupid about it?" I asked.

"You should stop moping around. Just come out and have a good time. That's why we're here."

I knew my cousin was right. I still adored him, in a helpless, forever way, and could imagine sitting side by side with him on the boardwalk steps, eating ices drizzled with syrup, knees touching. But too much had changed in the past year.

"I'll catch up with you later." As I left the table and went upstairs, I took pride in turning down the sultry temptation of putting on my buffalo sandals and cut-off shorts and trotting out of the garden with him to the boardwalk.

In my room I sat before my Smith-Corona, arranged my father's notes, which were stuck into the various pages of books, and puzzled over his scribbles. Numbers were the worst for me. I had never memorized those keys and had to slow down and resort to the tedious hunt-and-peck method. And this latest batch of notes was a mess.

In neat, careful sentences he told the story of Faraday's experiments. Then he described a man named James Maxwell, who through careful calculations invented an even stranger universe of fields of energy. Yet my father couldn't settle into the chapter. The equations were incomplete. He had written his own ideas in the margins, drawn arrows to the other men's ideas. *Descartes's plenum,* he wrote, *filling the sugar vat, is gone. Nothing is solid. Everything moves.* If I followed the hapless, loopy arrows, I found a fragment of an idea dropped here, picked up several paragraphs below, only to be crossed out. He couldn't decide on his argument; no one concept ignited him, each new route of thinking short-circuited into a frizzy tangle.

From my window, I could just make him out as he paced the

beach, absorbed in thought, brown foam chasing his ankles. He tossed a flat pebble, watched it sink. I imagined him running into the water, trying to plunge inside his own memories, back to that moment in the schoolhouse when he believed he had become light.

I stayed in my room and worked all through the morning typing my father's notes. After a while my back began to ache, and it felt as if bits of gravel were rubbing under my shoulder blades. I could hear voices drift over the hedges, what sounded like George and the soft trill of two girls. Envious, I squared my haunches on the chair, dropped my head, typed a few lines. The more I denied myself, the purer I felt. The typewriter soothed. I loved the notion that one day I would have what I wanted, a happy family, my father finally done with his work. For now, I would submit to this dark room with columns of books beside me.

"What are you doing indoors on such a beautiful day?" my uncle asked as I stepped outside, into the garden. Already Uncle Tom had persuaded the guesthouse landlady to let him "correct" her gardening. He was on his hands and knees before the flower beds, with shears, trowel, and twine laid out like surgical instruments on a canvas cloth.

"I'm busy. I'm helping my father."

"Nonsense. Last summer you were always playing outside, doing things, like with that boy Peter."

Even now, a year later, I could feel the crumbly calamine on my arms and cheeks, the shame that burned my skin.

"He's not a bad boy," my uncle added. "Truly."

I waited for him to say something more. He didn't. He patted the earth and shifted to another rosebush. That's the way
my uncle was. He let drop a few short, dry phrases, as if hoping
the meaning would slowly rise, moist with emotion. Half the
time I didn't even know what he was saying, but a faint vapor of
love seemed to cling to me. He was a good man, as my aunt said.

"What are you doing?" I asked.

"Checking for rot." He steered his arm around a forest of
thorny stems and tweaked off a few pink petals rimmed with
brown. "Once I tore up my whole garden after I found a few
tomatoes stricken with rot. Then I started again."

"The whole garden?"

"Too much rot and the whole thing's no good," he explained.

How different he was from my father. I watched him re-
sume his work, plucking spotted petals until he had gathered a
small, feathery pile near his knees. I admired his care, the way
he tested the remaining roses, brushed the fragile blooms with
his index finger so they wouldn't bruise. He held out a palm,
where a single petal balanced, its bowed center so translucent
that I could see my uncle's lined skin beneath. I wondered if I
could be as careful with my father's work, combing his notes for
the important ideas, knowing which passages to discard.

George's head popped over the hedge and he waved to me.
"Come on, you moody little snail. We've got to get going."

"Where to?"

"Your dad's treating us to fish and chips. Says he'll take us to
the park too if we want."

"Great!" My father hadn't offered to do such a thing in a
long time, ever since that first summer, when he'd spent too

much money on the family. He must be in a good mood, I thought, as I left my uncle and followed George out of the garden.

On the Palace Pier boardwalk, as I tossed the remains of my lunch into a wastebasket, a man eased toward me. "Hey, little lady." He smiled and yanked on the points of his black vest. "Out for a walk with your dad?"

"Yes." I took a faltering step back. George and my father sat on a bench a few yards away, finishing their fish and chips. My mother and aunt had gone to one of the saltwater pools; afterward they planned to rub grapefruit slices on their thighs and go for a vigorous walk on the beach.

Something about the man looked familiar, though—his knobby wrists, the long neck straining in collar—but the stomach was plumper than I remembered, and he wore black waiter's pants with satin stripes up the legs. Then I heard my father's shout: "Maywa!"

Maywa's mouth swept into a grin. "Yeah, man. It's me."

"What you doing here!"

It took a few minutes for the coincidence to sink into our minds. George and I signaled to each other, *It's another one of those funny folks who come around now and then with gold chains and greased-down immigrant taste,* and Maywa started doing what I remembered, that dodgy, quick-footed walk. He looked as if he wanted to move and stay still at the same time. "I'm just working here for the season until I make enough money," he explained breathlessly. "Saving up. Going to start university in the fall, yes I am, Warren, going to be a doctor."

His voice strained with earnestness, but I could see the yellow rum in his eyes, the missing teeth. It couldn't be, my father's expression said. His body went into a relaxed slump, his face softened, and he took Maywa in like lapping water. Maywa pulled on my father's arm. "Come on, man, let me take you to where I work! Is lots of fellows over there I want you to meet."

My father cast a nervous glance at the beach, where Uncle Tom and Timmy sat in deck chairs. "All right," he said, and the three of us followed Maywa down the boardwalk, into a huge, noisy restaurant, and then into a bustling kitchen, the floor slick with food scraps. In the rear, a man in a white jacket sat on a crate, skinning potatoes.

"Dr. Raj, take a look here," Maywa said to him, "this here my second cousin, Warren Singh! He from Berbice, man!"

The man wiped his hands on his trousers and stood. His hair made a thin, wispy crown, and the loose tan skin of his face was lined. There was a dreamy intensity to his eyes. He saw what lay in front of him and at the same time didn't see it.

"And look here, Warren," Maywa continued. "This is Seeraj Dripaul, but we call him Dr. Raj. He a real doctor, man, a psychiatrist, he fix people up good!"

Dr. Raj soberly took in my father and bent at the waist in a small bow. His sentences shifted between odd, stiff phrases and Guyanese talk. "Yes, after I received my degree I went back to practice, among my people. Of course, the situation, it has deteriorated terribly down there. Politics makin' that place crazy no doctor can cure. So for a while I'm doing some work here." He said this as though he had opened a clinic in the corner to treat the kitchen help.

"And how your family down there doin'?" Maywa asked.

"Not so good," my father replied. "My brother still in a bad way."

Dr. Raj squinted, suddenly placing my father. "Now I remember! You have two sisters down there, one of them a missionary?"

My father nodded.

"I went to visit once. Your sisters asked me to see if maybe I could help your brother. Such a nice family. They have your picture up on the wall, and another of your little girl, and they talk about how proud they are of you!"

His mention of our pictures made me queasy, as it always did when I remembered that in another place, another version of ourselves lived with my aunts and uncle.

Dr. Raj gave my father a knowing look. "I remember, at one time he such a strapping fellow. All us boys used to look up to him. So sad, so sad." He shook his head. "People like us, we carryin' a lot from down there."

My father winced. He didn't like to talk about Joseph.

Maywa gently slapped my father on the arm. "Warren here, man, he's goin' somewhere! He's a professor at some high-up place in America. One day he going to teach at Cambridge University. You should listen to him, man, all the things he writin' about, light and physics, it's so deep I can hardly keep track. He's a professor of light!"

Again Dr. Raj nodded. "This is very important work you're doing," he said in a serious voice. I noticed his pinky nail was extremely long. "Very important."

George and I rolled our eyes, and I put a hand over my mouth and stifled a laugh. My father inched closer, though I couldn't tell if this was out of interest or loyalty. I wished I could take him by the sleeve and lead him through the doors, back to the guesthouse, where he would be safe from people like this. Dr. Raj had only just warmed up. His arm swept across the room, as if to stroke the heads of the waiters and cooks.

"These English people, they don't understand. They are nearing the end of their civilization. We are the ones who have traveled. Did you know that the boats that took us from India to Guyana, they were called jihads? It was a holy journey we took. On those boats we became like brothers and sisters. No one on the same boat could marry, even after touching land. We understood. We knew the way to survive was to hold on to who we were and go forward." He made a hard fist, then slowly loosened his fingers, letting go a magic dust into the air.

"Warren, we need people like you. You do us proud. You got to be careful, though. Pardon my language, but you can't write no bullshit. Your pen, it got to cut like a sword, get to the real truth."

I noticed my father dab the corner of his eye. And even though George was shooting me quick, mocking looks, Dr. Raj had moved me too. He was more than a cook in a stained white jacket who stood in front of his crate, more than his words. Dr. Raj saw beyond the kitchen help washing lettuce leaves, beyond the dirty walls, and graced my family and Uncle Joseph with a sad beauty. We were special, we were the people of the jihad, couldn't George understand that?

As we made our way back to the beach, the sun was starting to lower in the sky; the amusement park rides looked like muted candy drops. We found my mother and Aunt Inez sitting with Uncle Tom and Timmy on the beach. "How was your walk?" Aunt Inez asked.

"Fantastic," my father replied.

I wondered if he was going to tell my aunt about running into Maywa and meeting Dr. Raj, or if he was afraid that telling about them would make the encounters evaporate like soap bubbles in the brisk sea air. I watched my mother reach for a jar of cocoa cream, hair spread across her sunburnt back. My father's eyes flickered with interest as he took in her pink-tinged shoulders sprinkled with gingery freckles. To my amazement, he grabbed the jar from my mother and lifted her hair from below, then held the brown strands aloft, studying them.

The moment was breathless, exquisite, my mother's hair buoyant as the waves behind. My father dipped his fingers in the jar and rubbed the cream on my mother's skin. He lathered her shoulders and arms as the late afternoon fell around us in a powdery-blue honeymoon haze.

If I hadn't been afraid that George might laugh at me, I would have jumped up from the blanket and done a little dance of celebration on the pebbles. There was my father, touching my mother, in public! What an extraordinary afternoon, running into Maywa on the boardwalk, the salt-clean air and fairy-tale minarets, this surge of hope. Maybe meeting Dr. Raj was good luck, after all. For the first time I believed in this holiday, and the possibility of change.

When the family came downstairs to breakfast the next morning, Dr. Raj was waiting for my father in the front parlor. He looked a little less rumpled and greasy than he had the day before, and his wispy hair was combed to a silvery thin tail. "I've brought some reading that I thought you'd like," he said in greeting. "That is, if you don't mind."

I watched my father carefully as he accepted Dr. Raj's books. I was worried. Yesterday's walk on the beach must have yielded no new ideas, for my father had brought me no fresh batch of notes to type.

"About your brother," Dr. Raj was saying. "Maybe I can help."

"Oh, no." My father's face shut with embarrassment.

Dr. Raj sidled close, almost breathing into my father's collar. "Think about it. I'm going back in a few weeks' time. I may be able to do some treatment at New Amsterdam Hospital, where I hope to have a clinic. In the meantime, you must come to my adda."

"What's an adda?" I asked.

"Every few nights," Dr. Raj explained, "several of us get together for a circle of talk, as they do in Bengal, under a banyan tree. Only here, we sit at the beach under the stars." He grinned at my father. "I hope you might join us."

"I might," my father said.

"You'll do nothing of the sort," Aunt Inez fumed a half-hour later, after my father told her about Dr. Raj's offers. "I know a fellow like that. He's just like Maywa. He's no psychiatrist. He'll hang a shingle in the village, say he's a doctor, and charge all those poor people."

"It's just talk," Warren said.

"Talk leads to money." She crisply cut her sausages into bite-sized pieces. "What about all those pounds you give to Maywa years back?"

Over boiled eggs and sausages, the adults ground through a familiar argument. Uncle Tom and Aunt Inez of course favored avoiding Dr. Raj and Maywa altogether, this was a *holiday*, after all. My mother's spoon tapped expectantly against the egg in its cup. An adda, a party, some excitement! I could see her calculate which dress she would wear. The red-checked with the crisscross back, or the apricot sheath?

That evening, after we took our lukewarm seven-minute baths at the guesthouse and put on fresh clothes for supper, my father and mother, George, and I set off across the beach to find the Brighton adda. The sea splashed in pleasant, burbling pools, tossed up stringy chains of seaweed. I was thrilled to see my father roll up his cuffs, tuck his arm under my mother's, and stroll along the beach like a teenager.

We found Dr. Raj, nestled in the slatted shadows of the amusement park fence on a throne of folded towels, as calm and pleased with himself as any banyan-tree philosopher. A circle of men was gathered around him, along with three hippie girls, the limp curtains of their hair parted to show moist, credulous eyes. The girls were a kind I disliked. They were seekers and believers, their edges were vague, like the frayed jeans and gauzy blouses all three wore.

"Come, come, Professor!" Dr. Raj greeted us. "We were just talking about the future of this little rocky island they call England." He pointed toward the gaudy boardwalk strip, the minarets of the Royal Pavilion. "This land of theirs, don't you see, it's changing, it's been changing for centuries. See those cliffs? Those fields behind? That's where the Romans and later the Saxon invaders came."

"That was Cornwall," I corrected.

He ignored me. "You think this land, these people will stay the same? Look closely. See all the brown faces on the streets, working in the kitchens, in the shops and schools, and like our professor here, teaching at some great university like Cambridge—"

"He hasn't taught there yet," I objected.

Raj shot me a glowering look. "Don't ever underestimate what your father is. This light your father is writing about, people from the jihads, we know. Our psyches are permeable. We know how to bend and adapt, we are like those light waves you write about."

I could see Maywa's grin, a gleaming crescent. "See what I mean, man? The doctor here, he deep."

"It's right there in the Upanishads." Dr. Raj began to recite: " 'Once the sun and moon have set, and the fire has gone out, and no sound is heard, what serves as man's light? The Self is his light, for by the light of the Self, man sits, does his work, and when his work is done, he rests.' "

"Be careful," my father countered. "There's nothing worse than a thinker who does not distinguish between the self that apprehends and the object that is being apprehended. That's blurring concepts. Occam's razor, man, the simplest answer to the facts is the best."

"Ah, but those medievalists were leading us to the tyranny of English empiricism!" Dr. Raj replied. "A plethora of concepts is our true inheritance. Even the ancient Greeks knew that these names we give to things are hollow vessels for a true reality."

The two men laughed, heartily, and the night blurred on. My mother rested her head on my father's shoulder. George and one of the Gauzy Girls brushed arms and talked in whispers.

Each hour melted into the next, and the brilliant hues of the amusement park rides reeled across the night sky. The talk was solid with facts, figures, and history, which dissolved into the vapors of epistemology and quantum physics. More people streamed across the beach and joined the adda: busboys, waiters, the local newsagent, and a few more hippies with their embroidered Guatemalan satchels.

Dr. Raj and my father were the center of attention, arguing and sallying back and forth. I was a little jealous, because their conversation was just like the dialogues he and I had on Horsendon Hill, but it thrilled me to see my father happy and animated. Now and then others joined in. They all wanted to tell their own stories; they all wanted to be more than they were, and were traveling into the heady ether of their dreams.

We stumbled back to the guesthouse at two in the morning. As I crawled into bed, I heard something on the other side of the wall, my parents' room. The sweep of bare feet on the floor, the metallic creak of a chair. I tensed. Then a familiar sound: scratch, scratch, my father's favorite pen on notecards, the cursive strokes flowing across the line. He was writing! I exulted. Snap! he turned the card. That night, I dreamed of flaming words riding the inky Brighton waves.

The addas became a ritual. Every few nights my mother fished out one of her pretty dresses from the closet and pressed it on a guesthouse towel with her travel iron. In our rooms, George and I scooped shillings into our pockets for playing the game arcades or going on a quick ride before the night began. Later, knock, knock, Dr. Raj appeared at the door, always in the same shirt and trousers, to pick us up. Aunt Inez, Uncle Tom, and Timmy never joined us.

On the boardwalk, Dr. Raj and my parents would stroll together while George and I brought up the rear. Often the wind sighed; the water drew black and silken amid the gray pebbles. I loved to watch Dr. Raj steady my father at the elbow, as if he were a patient, the one needing healing.

Now and then Dr. Raj talked about his own work, how he specialized in treating people like Uncle Joseph. Somehow my father's book on light corresponded to Dr. Raj's work with mental patients, though I couldn't quite follow. "Our history makes for extraordinary men," Dr. Raj explained. "Often, it's the extraordinary men who fall."

One week, ten days, two weeks, the holiday neared its close. Mornings, as the fog lifted, my father took me to the beach and pointed to the moving waves. Think of them as forces, he would tell me, carried across the world, to be caught by Joseph on the other side, pulling us into a great field of connection. His notecards came to me later, bound with a rubber band. *Tap-tap*, the onionskin pages accumulated on my desk, lifted with a rustle when a breeze blew through the window. Not quite a chapter, but getting solid. The atmosphere of the boardwalk talks shifted, ever so subtly. Some nights my mother didn't join us, and the two men would walk, Dr. Raj's grip on my father's elbow tighter, my father looking grateful for the touch. A secret floated between them.

"I don't like it," my uncle complained one afternoon as he and I kneeled before the roses. We were on his last project for the garden, thinning the bushes so the branches had room to grow. "Those people are talking rubbish. Your father shouldn't spend his time filling his head with all that grandiose claptrap. What kind of holiday is this?"

"My dad says Dr. Raj inspires him," I explained. "He's even thinking of showing him his book."

"Nonsense. Your father should get a proper read on his manuscript from a proper professor. Who is this Raj character? What are his credentials?" He snipped off a few slivered branches and neatly bunched them to the side. Veins of sunlight showed between the leaves.

"I think he just likes Dr. Raj," I said uncertainly. "He can relate to him, being from Guyana and all. And they know a lot of the same things."

"Everything is mixed up in this family," he continued. "Take these flower beds. You keep everything square and separate, and each plant flourishes on its own. Too close, the roots become tangled, and soon enough the whole lot of bushes is ruined."

"Dad says great ideas are born when two seemingly opposite or unrelated concepts are yoked together."

"Great ideas are born from clarity," my uncle said. "Tell me this. Has your father, by any chance, promised those people anything?"

I swallowed, throat dry. "No."

"Just remember what I told you about the garden. One bit of rot—"

"—and the whole thing is torn up again."

"You promise you'll tell me if something's afoot?" he asked, smiling.

I nodded, though I didn't really know what was happening, whom I believed more. My father was happy. He wrote, he took walks, my parents laughed. At night I could hear them through the wall, and imagine my mother's thin neck tilted back as she drank in her pleasure. I also felt a twinge of guilt. This holiday was my uncle's idea, after all. And now it was trickling through his fingers.

I liked to watch him tie the excess branches into bundles with twine, brush the dirt beds smooth. The garden already looked remarkably different. The wild, tousled bushes stood erect, the roses no longer drooped on their stems. I noticed also that his hands trembled when he reached for things; how lonely and stark the air of the garden felt.

Later, when I was back at my desk, my uncle's suspicions came to stain every page, seeped into my father's ragged sentences. *Grandiose claptrap. One bit of rot.* Which way of thinking was right? My father had always said that the beauty of real genius, real insight, lay in not being afraid to stare into the clamor of nonsense. I thought of the sun's rays bouncing off the white-hot pebbles, our adda nights, the octopus ride's whirl through the air. My father's chapter had not thinned to a single idea. New half-thoughts sprang up all over. In the past few days, Dr. Raj's phrases cropped up between Maxwell's elegant mathematics. The light of the self always transmutes. Electrons like people on the jihad, crammed together on the boats, scattering.

When I turned a card over, I saw a clump of numbers in a corner. I squinted, tried to tease out the formula. A shiver passed through me. I knew this wasn't a mathematical model. And before I could help myself, I set aside my work and sneaked into my parents' room. My fingers had a life of their own. They foraged in my father's accordion files and the extra papers kept by the nightstand, riffled through the books Dr. Raj had loaned him. They grew bolder. I shifted to the closet and dipped into his trouser pockets. I knew it was wrong. But I had to find out. And I discovered something, in the breast pocket of a shirt, warm as a slice of fresh-baked bread.

It was two pieces of paper, one folded into the other. The first was a bank slip, the numbers ghostly smudges. The other was one of the blue notecards he used for writing his chapter. More numbers, and this time I saw with complete certainty that they were currency calculations. Pounds, dollars, Guyanese dollars. The name *Seeraj Dripaul,* with an address for a bank in Guyana circled. Then *Joseph, Clinic,* underlined so many times the pen had torn through the paper.

George turned the bank slip over in his palm and studied its faint numbers. "I think it's for Uncle Joseph," I explained. "Dr. Raj is opening a clinic—"

"Don't be stupid. It's nothing like that. Why does your dad keep giving away his money? He's a fool."

"He is not!" I knew my cousin was partly right, but I was too mad at him. He and one of the Gauzy Girls—her name was Peg—were growing steadily more attached, she in those stringy cut-offs, he with his slender stride. They looked like two wind chimes that tapped against each other and let off sweet, tinkly music. "He has a big heart, that's all. He gave you a stereo and a bicycle, didn't he?"

George's eyes clouded with hurt. "This is different," he insisted. "Those people. They're weird." He handed the paper back to me. "I think we better have a talk with Dr. Raj."

At his boardinghouse, we found Dr. Raj sitting cross-legged on his bed, a cotton shawl over his shoulders; Maywa sat nearby on a wooden chair.

"It's always a delight to see Warren's daughter," Dr. Raj remarked, though his voice said otherwise. "What can I do for you?"

I hesitated. The room was soiled and small. There wasn't much furniture, just two single beds, a desk. How could this man be a psychiatrist, I wondered. But what did I expect, proof? And of what, his medical degree? There was nothing. Some restaurant receipts, a few books.

"Are you going to take my father's money?" I blurted, then wanted to bite back the words.

Two furrows appeared between Dr. Raj's eyebrows, and quickly smoothed out. "What makes you think such a thing, darlin'?"

"What about the clinic?" George demanded.

I half expected Dr. Raj to ignore me, as he often did. He stayed calm and reached for a beautiful silver pen and pad of paper. "Let me explain," he said. His manner was careful and slow. First he drew a map of where he planned to open his clinic in Guyana.

"Your father has a vision, Meggie. And you mustn't dismiss that vision. He's dealing with a fundamental paradox of the universe, that light is both a particle and a wave. Now your poor uncle Joseph, he was like that too, trying to go in two directions at once. And only someone like myself can offer the proper kind of treatment. I know what it's like to suffer the paradoxes of the soul."

I tried to listen as Dr. Raj spoke, but it was just like the chapter my father was writing—airy, pleasing, sparks whizzing across each card, tickling my brain. I couldn't pin down what he was saying. What did Uncle Joseph have to do with light? I grew discouraged, and the more I listened and watched him write on his pad, the more Dr. Raj began to resemble a gruesome cartoon character, a fun-house version of my father, his hair in crazy tufts. I felt dirty and small, as dirty and small as the room. George, my uncle, they were right. My father was a fool. He and I were nothing more than these shabby books with peeling spines, the broken-down house we could never really leave.

"I don't follow," I interrupted. "You're saying too many things at the same time!" I stamped my foot. "Who are you?"

Maywa spoke up from behind me. "Raj, man, leave her alone. She Yankee-born. She don't understand how it is with us."

"I want to understand!" I said, exasperated.

Dr. Raj folded his hands. "Darlin', it's time you should go."

I hated Maywa at that moment, hated the distant look in his narrowed eyes. That evening in the woods when I was afraid of him, he'd pushed me into the shadows so I couldn't belong to my father's world. I wanted to tell both him and Dr. Raj how I remembered the stories, how much I had helped my father, typing every afternoon until my back was sore.

I stormed out of the room. George called out for me, but I had plunged into the amusement park crowds. People jostled from all sides; a heavy girl with a mounded ice cream cone leered and licked. I went deeper into the clang and throb of arcade aisles. A tinny voice over a megaphone urged customers to shoot a plastic wild boar. Then I found what I was looking for: the ugly, alluring contraption of shiny metal and flashing bulbs that was the octopus ride. I watched the gangly green arms as they swung up, pitched the round seats high against the indigo sky, dropped them down again.

The ride again climbed in an elegant, graceful arc, paused, then shot down. I felt bits of myself spin from my body. Maybe it was I who was light, releasing a crackling shaft of energy as I carried my father to the shining future ahead.

Back at the guesthouse, the landlady handed me an envelope addressed to my father. Across the front were the words: *Thought this was important—John.* It was from my aunt and uncle's neighbor, John Gregory, who was keeping our mail. "No one else in your family is around," she said. "You'll see your dad gets this?" I tucked it into my pocket and went outside to sit on the guesthouse steps, where I opened the envelope. Inside, I saw, was a transparent envelope holding a telegram. I read, the words blurring:

Brother Joseph died last night. Pray for him.

For several minutes I looked at the churned-up gray sky, not sure what to do. Then I went to my father's bedroom and gathered the pages of his chapter, and returned downstairs and tied it with some of Uncle Tom's twine. I hurried with the packet to the beach, where I knew everyone was having a picnic. When my uncle saw me, he stood up from his chair and laid a cool hand on my wrist. "Tell me what's wrong," he said.

My words came out, but they were jumbled. Something about electrons, the jihad, magnetic waves, the telegram, Uncle

Joseph. I bit off the end of a sentence, started again. "The chapter," I sputtered. I pressed my fingers against my eyelids. I couldn't quite remember what went wrong first. The room, Dr. Raj, the silver pen. I knew I had to start at the beginning. "The clinic," I finally said.

"What clinic?"

I fished the bank slip from my pocket and waved it in the air. "I went to Dr. Raj to ask him about this."

My father stumbled toward me, alarmed, as Uncle Tom let go of my wrist. "Where did you get that?" my father asked.

"In your pocket."

"You betrayed me!" he thundered. "My own daughter, doing such a thing!"

I pressed the packet to my chest. A bleak shadow covered my thoughts, as if I had scribbled over my father's writing, smudged away his hard work.

"Warren, enough." My mother squeezed her hands into fists. "What's the truth here? Have you given them money?"

My father gazed wildly around the beach. I thought he might run into the water, try to swim to Guyana himself. "Look it here. Raj says he's going back. He says he can use the money to help my brother."

"Wait a minute," I protested. "There's more——"

"Don't do it, don't do it." Uncle Tom's words were tight whip-cracks of sound.

"I have to," my father said. "It's my brother. I promised! I promised a long time ago. You remember, Inez."

Aunt Inez paused, perhaps recalling that night when my father spoke to her from the gate and promised to take care of her.

When she spoke, her voice was soft, caressing. "Of course I remember, brother. And you been so good to me, over here. You going to let that promise ruin your life?"

The telegram was pulling my pocket down like a stone. *Tell him. Tell him.*

"You don't understand," my father said. "That man give me hope! What's so bad about that? He come here and pull me up and make me hope again for my brother!" He snatched the bank slip from my fingers. "You see this here?" he shouted. "This is mine. *My* money. If that going to help my brother, if that going to make the bad voices go away, I got to do it!"

"No!" I yelled. "Everyone, please be quiet!"

All eyes turned to me. I handed the telegram to my father. He read it, once, twice, three times, eyes darting from side to side. He stumbled backward in the sand. He didn't cry. He didn't say anything. He simply handed the telegram to Inez and stood in silence. No one could move. Gulls dove and flew off. We were surrounded by a vacuum of sound.

My mother put her arms around my father's shoulders and said quietly, "You know, Warren, in many ways, Joseph's life was over a long time ago."

Tears streamed down his cheeks. "I know. I always thought, God, yes, maybe he would get better. Maybe I could save him."

We stayed on the beach for a long time, as the sun lowered and the ocean turned a purplish-blue. One by one, my family repacked the straw hamper, folded chairs, and drifted away, until only my father and I remained on the damp pebbles. A strong wind blew, thinned the clouds. The sea pulled in, drew back; the day was sorting itself out, breaking up the old connections. First the news of Joseph's death. Now this manuscript, which I still clutched to my chest, its edges curled in the moist air.

My father said, "What next, my dear?"

I was flattered that he'd asked. But I was also prepared. The weight in my arms grew heavier, dense with all I'd learned. I remembered that night during our first summer in Sudbury when I'd watched the ashes fall over the rooftops, and that evening in the woods with my father and Maywa. It was I who could wade between the forking paths, stories and reason, nonsense and logic.

I stood up, shook off sand. "Dad, it has to go."

He didn't seem to hear. I edged forward. The pebbled ridge gave way to sand, and eased into dark green waves. I heard him call out, "What are you doing?"

I kept walking, the water shocking cold around my ankles. "Meggie!"

Calmly I turned around. My father had run up from behind; his trousers billowed into sacks. "What are you doing?" he gasped.

I touched the manuscript. "You need to start again, Dad. It's all mixed up. You're trying to say too many things at once."

"Darling, it's a rough draft, that's all."

I loosened the twine, and a few pages spun into the froth and were swiftly lost. I imagined them reaching Guyana, where Joseph was no more.

"Please!"

When I turned to him, my father's eyes rested on me. I could feel the air balance between us. The waves surged and ebbed. One word, one false word, and I could release a vibration, a stirring of energy. I could blow the hope right back into him. One minute passed, and another, and soon I was strong in my resolve. It was a good thing, letting go. In one graceful motion, I flung the chapter into the ocean. There was a snap of whirring white. Then silence, as the pages floated on the sea and were carried away.

*With each leave-taking there is an imaginary trunk, where
everything must be locked away. Bharat Singh carried his
chappals, his tunic, his teak bowl, and his amulet and sailed from
the Bay of Bengal, off the edge of what he knew.*

*His daughter's trunk is sealed with ingot clasps and leaden
nails. Inside is the straw hat she wore on the boat over, rimmed
with a Scotch-plaid ribbon, a hole where the dried hibiscus
flower was once pinned. Her linen skirt is lined with a crusty
thread of blood. Jumbled in the center is her faded boat ticket,
the crushed aerograms she never sent home. Plum-stained
handkerchiefs are crammed into the corners.*

The Professor *of* Light

The boy has a cool, silent trunk, where he locks away his fears. His father's sugar crystals sparkle like gems against a dark silk lining. In its folds is his mother's coconut oil and betel nut scent; the thick nub of her braid rests on his pillow, twisting in the currents of his dreams.

In his new home he does not fall into the blue ache of nothing. He lives in a world bare as a monk's cell. He has only his books, his lost family, their hopes are fastened safe inside him. New things drop into his mind. He tries to put them away too—the gray North American sky, a wind that cuts like whips against his cheeks, a woman with a halo of hair framed in a Brooklyn apartment window. Her insect-bright eyes tease him. There is too much clutter.

Once, long ago, a young Albert Einstein dreamed of an imaginary trunk for an unimaginable knowledge. Inside his trunk he stowed a falling apple, the nooks and crannies of an empty room, a sliver of a clock hand.

What envy and awe the boy felt, for Einstein's was the real leave-taking. He traveled into a sunspot of fevered dreams, through alpine air, where the ether melted into another realm. There, Einstein saw himself astride a great beam of light. He looked over, and saw another ray moving at the exact same speed. The sky buckled. Time caved into ravines. Light stitched across the universe in a golden seam, touched each craggy moment.

Einstein dreamed so far that he created another trunk. The elegance of its architecture! An endless vault of photons and quarks, and through another opening, a mysterious essence, unknowable, always outside the boy's line of vision. His hands push, widen the sides to hold the beauty of paradox, crystal and liquid.

Inside this trunk Schrödinger's famous cat crouches, whirling through a midnight-blue firmament. Unseen to anyone, a random event—the radioactive decay of an atom—may set off a gas that kills the cat. We keep spinning through time and space, never knowing whether the event occurred. At any given moment, different versions of the cat exist in the universe, both dead and alive.

A man might be a thousand men. Each line creasing his palm, every seed he plants in a cane field, every story he tells holds a different vision of what he might be. Atoms burn electric, arrange themselves into flowering combinations. The sky is gorgeous with color, one story blooms into another, like the blue-skinned Shiva branching into a thousand avatars.

Look once more. There is a bench, high on a hill, in a slumbering London suburb. The boy has become a philosopher king, his daughter a little sage. Night after night they circle the bench, touch its rough edges, peer from all sides, try to hold each angle in their minds. Their voices mingle in the dark, fused like ancient stars. They dream as one.

Open the fruit of their talk, and find the girl curled around the knots and fissures of her father's mind. See his thoughts stamped on every cell of her skin. If she were to leave, they would leave as one. Together they would tumble off the edge, spin into a thousand flames, joined in their mystery box of questions.

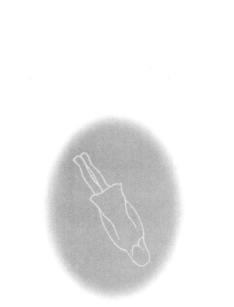

Seeing

After Uncle Joseph died, something began pulling in our Sudbury house. It was under the floorboards, a damp sadness that shaded our eyes, snuffed out hope. My father walked with a stoop, as if carrying the past and the future on his back. An unclean, stale air hung about him. Behind his spectacles were circles of ash.

The letters from Guyana became more desperate. *It's time you made good on your promise,* Aunt Edith wrote. *This is your home and it is falling apart. The stairs need fixing. The shutters are falling off. And what of our niece? Here she is almost grown up, and we don't even know her. Don't forget us, brother.* My father never answered his sisters, though I often saw him stand frozen by his desk, a letter dangling between his fingers.

He and I kept on with his new chapter, on quantum physics. It wasn't going well. He always closed the heavy green drapes and locked the door. I sat on the bed, poised with pen and pad, and watched him dash back and forth in the dark room. "Anything is possible. Reality melts," he proclaimed. "There's just quantum jumping, endlessly moving." His words shot from his mouth in a nervous blind streak, to die a moment later. Nothing burned hot and strong enough to take us further, over the edge of what we knew.

"So how come you don't answer Auntie Edith's letters?" I asked once.

He looked at me blankly; I might have been a student who had just posed a puzzling philosophy question. "It's the black water," he answered.

"What's that?"

"In Guyana, we have what we call 'black water.' That water is dark as night. Anytime you look into the water trench, you see only yourself, shining back like a ghost. They say if you drink that water, no matter where you go in the world, you have to come back home."

"That's disgusting!"

"No, Meggie. That black water is the sweetest water you ever taste, rich and belly-fillin'. But you got to be careful. That's what happen to Joseph last summer. One night he sneak out of the house. He want to taste that water, but he fall in the trench by the gate. There he lie until the sun come up, and my sisters find him gone from us.

"In quantum theory, we have what you call matter and anti-matter," he went on. "For every molecule that goes forward in time, there's another that goes backward. In this world, there are those who stay put and those who move on. My friend Arun, those fellows in Cambridge, they know I'm just a barefoot boy coming from that little place, like my brother. That's why it's time to leave the family here in Sudbury too. Otherwise I can't see clear into my own work, I cannot cross the black water and go forward."

Two summers before, a fever had burned the wet longing out of me, left a hard nugget of devotion. Now I was strong as forged metal. Ever since that time with Peter Whyte, I was able to steer clear of boys or throw a chapter into the sea, as I had done the previous summer. I'd become odd, not like my cousin, who'd blossomed into a handsome boy, with silky black hair curling to his collar; not like the girls back at my school, who walked in mincing steps on platform shoes. I might dress the same as they did, in bleached jeans and rayon print shirts, but you could see the stamp of Sita on my face, a flame in my eyes. I gave of my-self in another way. Like Aunt Didi, I stayed close to home. I knew the scratch of my father's pen on paper, the curve of his thoughts.

My vision made me different too. I had first noticed a change one day the past spring in math class, when the numbers on the blackboard faded to faint lines. Sometimes I relished my new way of seeing, how a room full of faces could look like lamps in twilight. When I finally was fitted for glasses, the optician's shop pinched into a box of detailed perfection. Counter edges sparkled. I experimented with the crisp outline the glasses made of the world, the way objects blurred when I swiveled my head.

In Sudbury, I began to observe other changes. My mother

and my aunt, who once had done everything together, now had nothing to say to each other. At breakfast, whenever my aunt asked what they should make for supper, my mother's response was, "I don't know." Then she would add, in a grave, burdened voice, "I'm too tired to think about that right now."

Every morning I came downstairs to find bedding on the sofa, my father's slippers in a corner. My mother was already dressed, in one of her beautiful suits, high heels and stockings, and she trailed the tart scent of perfume. Later she sat in the garden and flipped restlessly through magazines. Sometimes she went into the city for hours on end, without telling us where she'd been, exactly. When she returned, she shut herself in their bedroom, which she took over every night, leaving my father to sleep on the sofa downstairs. I could see her, luminous as a bottom stone, her long body flung across the bed, her face buried in the pillow as she quietly wept.

At night I saw the ghost of Joseph hunched by the rosebushes, ready to drag my father into his swampy trench. Aunt Edith and Aunt Didi were perched on the brick wall, chattering gray spots, always needing. In the morning I listened to my father's talk of quarks and photons. I knew the formula $E = mc^2$ from his index cards. My eyes had to do more. They had to gather the nighttime flecks, the subatomic bits lodged in the crevices of my father's mind. I must fuse them into a dark core of power, stop my mother in her pull away from us. And I must help my father see through the black water, to the other side.

"Absolutely not," my mother answered when my father proposed that the next year when we came to England he and I spend the summer in Cambridge. He handed her a form titled "Special Fellows Program, Trinity College," for the same fellowship Arun had won years before. If accepted, my father would be given use of the libraries, his own carrel, and a chance to lecture on the topic of his book.

"It's bad enough that I've given up so much for you, Warren," my mother said. She looked so sensible, planted in the center of the room in her new pin-striped dress. "Now you want to keep her in some college library all summer? She's a growing girl, Warren. She has to get out. That's why I told George that Meggie would love to join him at a party. It's on Friday, the night after Sheila arrives."

"Ma! How could you say that without asking me?"

"Wait a minute," my father objected. "Since when does Meggie go to parties with boys?"

"Since the dark ages ended. We're not raising Meggie as if she's in Guyana." My mother handed the form back to him. "Which reminds me. Have you written to your sisters?"

My father grew flustered. "It's no good. I have to stay away. Their vengeful spirits came for Joseph. Now they coming for me."

"No more superstitious talk." She headed for the door. "Just say that it's time they sold the house. We all need to get on with our lives."

The door closed. My father and I knew what she really meant to say: leave. She would leave my father if things didn't change. I tested the word in my mouth. Leaving wasn't for us. In our house, family was for life. My grandmother put letters in Joseph's pockets that became stones and brought him back home. Or she planted eggs under the stairs, turned Didi's yearnings into bird-ghosts. And if you leave with a promise unfulfilled, you are always leaving.

I could imagine, far away, in Guyana, the house stilts soften with longing. The parlor filled like a lake, dark water rising to the drapes. It tasted sweet, like sugar peas, and as my father made his way toward me, feet heavy, I could see him grope for balance. The moment his fingers touched my shoulder, the damp cold pricked my scalp.

"Help me get to Cambridge," he said. "Think of all we can do. We can work in peace, finish the book. I know I'm an old fool. But it will be perfect, Meggie. Just the two of us."

"You're not old," I said.

"I hear them, Meggie. I know you do too. My brother, he's still in the trench. My sisters trying to call to me. The spirit, it's in this house. Your mother's just like the other women, trying to hold us back."

His words spun in troubled spirals to the muddy depths of his mind. He wasn't making sense. This was happening more and more these days.

"Next summer," he insisted. "Next summer we must leave this house of women."

I felt his breath on my neck, the soothing touch of his hand on my hair. "Temptation," he whispered as he let me go. "You're being tested, Meggie. The women trying to claim you too. And you have to choose."

Sheila set down her luggage just inside the parlor. Her brown eyes flashed in my direction. "What a beautiful girl you're turning into, Meggie. But what's with this T-shirt and shorts?"

"If only you knew," my mother said. "Meggie is the essence of duty. I can't even get her to go to a party tomorrow night with her cousin. Can you imagine, a teenage girl who doesn't want to go to a party?"

From her pocketbook, Sheila brought out a dark red wooden box. "Take a look at what your aunt Edith has sent you." When I opened the lid, I saw a flap of blue velvet. Below gleamed two bangles, made of a pinkish gold, their rims cut with triangular facets.

"Uh-oh," Aunt Inez warned. "My sister is trying to bribe us into helping them both. Be careful, Sonia. Edith may be a missionary, but she's best at persuasion when it comes to money."

"Why are there two?" I asked.

The lid banged shut.

"In Guyana, when a girl bleeds the first time, the women in her family take two locks of her hair and dip them in her menstrual blood. Then they put the locks of hair in a black-water lake, where they turn into perfect gold bangles. This way, the girl's blood will flow away from her, yet she can still come back to herself. One bangle is the wish for a good husband, and the other is for many children.

"Only I got a different idea." Sheila winked. "The first bangle is to catch some boy's gaze. And the other is to please your own."

I squirmed as Sheila brushed her cold cheek on mine. I knew I should be grateful to her for bringing these bangles. But I could also hear my father's warning words about the danger of womanly illusions.

Sheila slipped the bangles onto my wrist. "There! Now we'll get Meggie ready for the party tomorrow."

Upstairs, I stripped down to my underwear while Sheila examined me, her long hands brushing my skin. One finger pressed my right hip. "The good thing is, she's not as hairy as the rest of us," she commented. "We should fix those legs, though. That way when the hair grows in, it'll be soft and fair." She bent my left arm and pointed to the black crease where the upper and lower parts touched. "See how dark it can get? You must be careful to stay out of the sun."

"I like to read in the sun!"

"Hush. Too much reading and you'll get an ugly squint and twitch in your eyes. Then you going to say, 'Me eye jump.' "

"What's that mean?"

"That means a spirit passed through your eye," Sheila answered.

I touched the side of my face. Did she know about the things I was seeing, ever since my eyes had gone bad?

Sheila spread a white chemical-smelling cream on my face and neck. A few minutes later, with a damp washcloth, she wiped it off, expert as a cat's tongue licking a bowl clean. Then she took coconut slices from a plastic bag and dipped them in a bowl of lemon juice. She glided the slices on my arms until the skin glistened like wet silk. I trembled with pleasure.

"This will help you keep your lovely color," she explained. I held my arms out and admired their smooth golden sheen.

From her suitcase Sheila brought out a round tin of wax, which my mother went to heat in a double boiler downstairs. I lay on newspapers spread on the floor. My legs prickled hot as she ladled the softened wax and flattened a cotton strip on top. When she tugged, a flame seared up my calf. I thought she had torn off my skin. When she ripped off the cotton, I put my fist in my mouth and swallowed the hurt.

"Beauty is pain," Sheila told me as I lay on the newspapers, shuddering and burning. The discarded strips, now coated with fine hairs, each crowned with a root, made me queasy.

To my dismay, my mother and Sheila began to gossip about the family, especially about my father and his careless ways. "It's so unfair," my mother said. "He spends his time laboring over that fellowship application and he can't write a short note to Edith. Now these gifts arrive and I haven't the foggiest idea what to do."

"You know Indian men, Sonia. They're impossible. Once they marry you, all they care about is their stomach."

"Or their work," my mother added.

"But Daddy needs to finish!"

My mother gave Sheila a rueful look. "Meggie always takes her father's side because he's so smart and charming. Wait until she learns a thing or two about what lies behind all that brilliance."

They turned away from me and I stayed on the newspapers. I hated that knowing tone in my mother's voice, hated how the two of them made me feel there was something peculiar in my protests, or in helping my father finish his book.

"Hearing from Edith this time reminds me of our one trip down there," my mother went on. "I stayed with Warren's sisters. They looked so old to me, yet Edith was only thirty-five! These poor women, all in a house in a village, no men to love. What anger I heard! Warren's mother wouldn't even let us sleep in the same room."

Sheila's hair had fallen over her cheek, her eyes moist. "That's the way our family was down there. Always holding you back. They don't want to listen to the sounds of another woman's pleasure."

I recalled the story of the red ribbon tied around my aunts and my mother and grandmother. In my mind the ribbon turned to a black vine that covered the walls and twisted around my wrists and ankles. My eyes swam with tears. This was not a story I wanted to hear.

"I was miserable," my mother said. "Warren spent all his time in his room trying to do his work. After a month I couldn't take it anymore. I sneaked into his room and we spent the night together. A few weeks later, I realized I was pregnant." My mother touched my bare foot. "Remember, Megan, dear? We used to tell you the story of the little bird that came and visited my belly in Guyana and carried us home?"

"No, I don't," I replied. I remembered all too well. It was the story of the blood of leaving. I didn't feel like smiling now, for the story didn't seem a happy one. The image of my mother hovering in my father's doorway made me uncomfortable. I must be different. I must be strong, like the hard pink gold on my wrist, a bright intelligence shining through.

"Your turn." Sheila pointed to my mother, who had already undressed.

Wrapped in a towel, my mother lowered herself onto the newspaper. She didn't cry out when Sheila tore off the strips. A raw flush stained her calves. Her hips and breasts shook.

Sheila spoke soothingly as she ran her palm down my mother's leg. "Enough of that sad talk, love. We've got to get out like Megan. Have ourselves a grand time."

"Mmm." My mother buried her face in her arms, and her calves tightened with the next rip of cotton.

I didn't like the mother I now saw. Stones of bitterness fell from her mouth. Sheila gathered them into her long fingers.

The air glinted with rage. Bare knees pulled to my chest, I could not stop shivering.

A few hours later I found my father sitting alone in the back parlor. He was wearing his red silk robe, and a good tie was knotted around his bare neck. He'd slicked back his hair with Brylcreem.

On the table was the application, and a deck of playing cards. "Hello, darling, I was waiting for you," he said. "It's time for the party."

I smiled. "Daddy, the party's tomorrow."

"Oh, that. The real party is right here." He shuffled the cards, cracked them against the edge of the table. "Just the two of us. A private party. There's so much to do. We have to dance. We have to talk and play games. Isn't that right?"

I sat opposite him, a strange flower of excitement opening in me.

"This is a game of probability." He pulled out a card. It was the ace of diamonds. "A single choice, but with too many possibilities." He waved the card. "Is it probable that Arun will talk to me if I call him? Or do you think he'll stop me from applying to Cambridge?"

"Daddy, Arun wants to help you."

"You know very little, Meggie. You should pay closer attention to what your daddy wants." He put the card back, shuffled the deck. "Pick a card," he ordered.

I turned one over. The jack of spades, an embroidered sash across his chest.

"Aha!" my father said. "Is it probable that you will be like a boy and become a scientist?" He wrote something down on the form. I felt as if I'd failed a test. He pointed again to the deck.

"Pick another one."

This time I turned over the five of clubs.

"Numbers. Perhaps you will be a great mathematician, better able than I to solve these problems." His eyes were cold. "Pick again," he commanded.

"Dad—"

"Pick!"

My hand shook as I lifted a card from the middle of the deck. It was the queen of hearts.

My father began to laugh. "Ha! The joke is on me." He tilted his chair, rubbed his cheek. "So you will be like that damn Sheila with her airs and perfume! You are like your mother with her treacherous ways!"

He pulled at the bangles on my wrist. "Your aunties send these to you? Is that what I raise you to be? No more than a common girl with her flashy gold? Like my sisters, grabbing, always wanting?"

"Leave me alone," I begged. My wrist burned.

"Temptation," he declared. "There are so many byways, leading us in the wrong directions. Who knows what path you'll take. Last summer you almost destroyed everything I'd worked for."

"You said I helped you."

"No one can help me. I'm all alone. I've always been alone." He let go and turned his back to me. "Leave me be," he said. "I have no time for this family and its foolish women. I have work to finish."

I wanted to do something mean, like toss his cards in the air and storm out of the room. Instead I went to put my arms around his shoulders, press myself into the doughy warmth of his stomach. But my hands froze in midair. Something about my father repelled me. A sour musk drifted from his clothes. With his unshaven cheeks, his angry talk, he was taunting me to stay away. And, I feared, it was working. I did not know how to make him see me.

The evening was damp and warm when George and I set out for the party. I'd put on a pair of hiphugger jeans, a stretch top that showed a glimpse of brown stomach, and a dab of gloss on my lips. I felt I'd been frosted in a sweet glaze, but I liked it too, especially when I shook my wrist and the bangles made a delicious clink.

At the rise of Horsendon Hill, I put a hand on my cousin's arm. "Let's run to the top and roll down, like we used to," I suggested.

"We can't. We're late."

"It's just a party, right? It doesn't matter what time we get there. We'll arrive all windblown and mysterious."

As if imagining himself this way, George took a comb out of his hip pocket and smoothed down his hair. Vanity was a trait I couldn't stomach in this new George. He quickened his stride until I called out to him, "Stop! I feel sick and you're walking too fast." I sat down on a nearby rock, clutching my side.

George joined me on the rock and lit a cigarette. This George smelled like a man, of tobacco and cologne, and was full of big flashy smiles, slaps on the back, a sway in his hips when he teased me. What lay inside him I didn't know anymore; no longer could I reach in his head and pull out his thoughts, make them funny.

We sat there a few minutes. George stubbed out his cigarette and got up. I stared at his strong back, the murky gray that spilled around him. The air grew more porous, busy with a sparkle I still couldn't explain.

"George," I asked, "do you believe in destiny? You remember how my dad used to talk about Uncle Joseph and the jumbee curse?"

"Meggie, Uncle Joseph was just an old drunk. Mum says all of them who stayed down there ruined their own lives."

I touched my chest. "But I have this feeling, ever since Uncle Joseph died. Right here. About all of us, George. Not just Joseph. Now it's growing bigger and trying to tell me something. I'm trying to figure out *my* own destiny," I added under my breath, but he didn't hear.

Hands stuffed in his jeans pockets, George began to pace, his body arched like a sail toward the party's curve, its warm, less introspective voices. "Are you feeling any better? You sound it."

"Yes," I replied. "And no."

"Why are you so confusing tonight?"

Because *I'm* confused, I almost blurted. Because there you stand, crisp as a movie star with your new shoulders, not afraid of the separate paths we are moving on. I stood and slipped my hand under his arm, amazed by the hard muscle beneath his cotton sleeve. We walked arm in arm, me stumbling in his athletic strides. Darkness fell about us, woolly and thick. But it was also good, leaning on George.

"You all right, little cousin?" he asked when we reached the end of the woods.

"Yes," I answered. "Only go a little slower, please."

At the party, dozens of kids milled about the small rooms, drunk and sweaty. A few boys, stripped to their undershirts, showed the fleshy pink of their chests. I picked up a bottle of Guinness from a rubber tub piled with ice and beer, and George tried to introduce me. After a while people avoided me, since I didn't want to dance.

Jillie, a tall, willowy girl, took pity on me. "We can dance together," she offered.

"I couldn't do that to you." I squeezed my silver mesh purse, felt the bumpy contours of my glasses inside.

"What do you mean?" She smiled.

"It's just that I'm—"

"Stubborn," a voice put in. "Meggie is one of the most stubborn girls on the face of the earth."

A fist might have jabbed me, quick, in the ribs, I was so surprised. Peter Whyte stood before me. Greedily, I took in every bit of him. He wasn't plump anymore, but lanky and tall. His blond hair was cut into a feathery shag and he wore wire-rimmed glasses. His eyes, though, were the same fierce blue.

"I'll leave you two to your squabbling," Jillie said, and sidled away. We retreated out the back door to the cool quiet of the garden.

"How is it I never see the ever-elusive Meggie Singh?" he asked as he sank next to me on a bench.

I sipped my beer, hoping it would cool the flush on my

cheeks. It was a long time since I'd sat this close to Peter. I remembered lying on the moist ground two summers before, the tickle of leaves on my neck.

"I'm busy all the time with my dad," I told him. "I don't know how to help him anymore, though. He's talking about us going to Cambridge next year. My mom thinks that's a really bad idea."

Chin on his fists, Peter was silent for a moment. "Tell me this. What did you do for your father before?"

I shrugged. "Type his notes. Organize things. Stuff."

"That won't do. If you want someone to pay attention to what you're saying, you have to do it in a big way. My dad's a busy man. It's only when I challenge him at the supper table that he even notices. You have to take a stand. Make it dramatic. You can't just be a little peon. Your dad will respect you more if you stand up to him."

"Really?"

"Truly."

We watched the other kids dance inside, their silhouettes pirouetting across the open window. I liked the solid curve of Peter's shoulders, fingers in his lap. But I was skittish, not sure what to do with my own hands. I fumbled inside my purse for my glasses, and found them in a crooked line, one stem stuck upward.

"Oh, dear," Peter said. He placed the glasses on me, bent stem poking over my left ear. "That's lovely. They make you look awfully smart."

He stroked the side of my face, which confused me. My glasses made me want to look at him, yet his touch made me think about myself. Peter's mouth searched my face. His cheek tasted cold. His lips were on mine, his tongue darted along my teeth, and I let out small gasps of pleasure.

As Peter bent down and kissed my neck, I had the urge to strip off my top, have his tongue circle the burning seeds of my nipples. My own hands moved, touched where I might feel skin. Our chins knocked. His fingers inched up my ribs. But when I pulled off my glasses, the old sadness churned up. Bathed in the darkness, I thought of my father holding me tight that night in the garden when he rubbed my feet with dirt. I snatched my purse and glasses.

"What the hell—"

"Shit. I can't do this."

"Where are you going?" he called as I bolted from the bench.

I had already fled down the path, smoothing my top. In the living room, boys and girls swayed, bodies pressed close. Peter's shouts wound through the music. I found the front door and pushed through a crowd of kids smoking on the stoop. Then I began to run, hard.

When I reached our gate, I saw three figures staggering down the road. It was Sheila and my mother, each holding the arm of a man. My mother's long jacket flapped open, revealing a pale knee. "Hey, girls!" the man yelled. "Give a fellow a chance! Come on over to my place, it's just around the corner!"

They halted, a playful mirth on their faces. "Oh, Meggie," my mother said, laughing.

Our front door swung open. Crowned by the overhead lamp was Aunt Inez, her hair in plastic curlers. She resembled the photos I had seen of my grandmother, anger thick on her brow. She thrust her head out of the door, aluminum clips glinting, and shook a fist. "Do you know what time it is, making such a ruckus, waking the neighbors?" she asked.

The two women burst into laughter. "Go on!" Sheila gave the man a push, and he went spinning into the road. "I love you!" he shouted into the night air. "I love you-ou!"

Uncle Tom was there too, his hair standing in reddish tufts. As Sheila, my mother, and I headed upstairs, my aunt asked, "And what of my brother? What's he going to say to all this?"

Halfway up, my mother whirled around. Her mouth opened. I could tell she was about to say something sharp. She nodded in the direction of the parlor door. "You know he's always asleep by this hour."

But he wasn't there. He was in the garden, asleep in a chair, papers spread across his lap. Without a word, Uncle Tom woke him up and led him into the parlor. I loved my uncle at that moment, loved his discretion, how, I knew, he would fold up the chair and put away the papers, and never say a word about this.

Upstairs, Sheila ducked into my room, where she was sleeping, and my mother and I went into the bedroom she used to share with my father. "Silly, silly, silly," my mother said as she pulled off her dress and wobbled toward the bed. She hadn't even washed off her makeup. "We are all so silly," she repeated as she eased under the covers and rolled over, showing me her back, the faint puckers where the straps of her slip dug into her shoulders. "Did you have a nice time at your party, dear?" she asked.

I undressed, climbed into bed, and leaned against her. The odor of liquor drifted from her hair. "Where'd you go?" I asked.

"I was out with Sheila."

"But who was that man?"

She plumped a pillow. "Come, now. Let's be good bunnies and get some shut-eye."

I watched my mother until her breaths grew steady and long. My hands stroked my newly waxed legs, the soft skin over my ribs, where Peter had touched me. Was that wrong, what I'd felt at the party? And wasn't she worried about my father sleeping in the garden?

For a while I stared into the dark room. Black water spilled in a shiny tumble from my mind, branched to the window. I could feel my aunts stroke my wrists, curl tight into my thoughts. *We are joined to you,* they whispered. *Please bind your father back to us.* I woke, my pillow damp. The window was filled with water. I saw the white ovals of my mother's heels as she swam away from us, kicking up a spiteful froth.

"Where are you going?" I wanted to cry.

The answer seemed to lie in the secret creases of my mother's half-turned profile, one topaz earring still dangling from a lobe. She knew something, and it was buried where I could not see.

The next morning I found my mother at the breakfast table, drinking coffee. She looked rumpled and lost, kimono drawn tight around her breasts. Her hands trembled when she lifted her cup to her lips. "God, my head aches," she said to herself. "Who *was* I last night?" When she saw me standing in the doorway, she made a pouting face and held both arms out. "Come, sweetheart. Give your terrible lush of a mother a nice warm hug."

I curled into her lap of wrinkled silk. Though it was she who looked terrible, it was I who felt battered inside. "I thought I'd take you for a little shopping spree today," she said. "You looked so pretty and grown-up last night. We'll buy you some new clothes."

"Does Daddy know?" I asked.

Her voice was brusque. "He's busy with other things today, dear."

That afternoon the air shifted, and I saw a different mother trail through the London streets and stores, more lighthearted, younger. She loved to peer at merchandise in the glass counters, talk to salesgirls about the latest hem lengths, ponder the difference between two wool-and-rayon blends. From the racks she picked out skirts and sweaters of heather gray, russet, creamy satin. I could see myself on the Cambridge campus next year, dressed like a real college girl.

Then she flourished a striking outfit. It was a suede vest sewn with crocheted squares. Braided strands of yarn hung from the bottom, weighted by small beads. There was also a ribbed turtleneck, and shorts made of the same crocheted material, a thin lining inside. It reminded me of her afghans, cut into colorful pieces.

"Isn't it adorable?" she asked.

"Ma, I can't. I'll look like I'm wearing a blanket."

She twisted the vest off its hanger. "Oh hush, Miss Grumpy-Head. I know you're above trivial things like dressing nice. You want to be with your father, up in his clouds."

"What's wrong with that?"

Her eyes filled with tears. She banged down on a stool and rummaged for a tissue. "It's fine, Megan. But that means I have to keep my feet on the ground, isn't that right? Who's supposed to take care of writing your aunt Edith? Who keeps the family together?"

"He isn't so bad——" I said, then halted. A sadness washed through me. Maybe she was right. Maybe my father's work on his book had gone on too long. In the bright cube of a dressing room, I saw the beautiful woman who had once shorn her hair to elope and now found herself always alone. I imagined rubbing the cheerful shine off her cheeks to find her skin dusted with a cold powder of hate, her bones worn thin from waiting too long.

"Go ahead, dear," she urged. "Make your mother feel better. Try on this cute little outfit."

I pulled on the turtleneck and stepped into the hot pants, which were surprisingly smooth inside. I liked the suppleness of the vest, the bounce of the beads against my waist.

"Darling, don't squint like that. Sheila's right, it looks ugly. Put on your glasses."

When I put them on and saw myself in the mirror, I was embarrassed. The turtleneck hugged my breasts, made them bulge. The shorts, with their little holes, showed the curves of my thighs. Too much clutter stuck to me—the yarn fringes, the bangles. I remembered my aunts stroking my wrists the night before. *The women trying to hold us back,* I heard my father say.

"What do you think?" my mother asked. Her eyes were dreamy and wet.

"I'm sorry, Ma. I don't want it."

Small tears, like freshwater pearls, showed on her lashes. "Are you sure?" Her hand lingered on the squares of wool.

"I'm sure," I replied. As I unhooked the vest, the yarn caught on one of my bangles. I tugged and the vest came loose; beads tapped against the mirror. We watched as it slid like a stiff skin to the floor.

"Sonia? Sonia, is that really you?" a voice called out. It was brisk, American and New Yorkish.

My mother and I looked up from our restaurant booth, shopping bags mounded on the seat. A man in a navy blazer came toward us. For a second I thought he was one of my father's colleagues. Then my mother's voice rang with astonishment. "Hiram?"

"My God, Sonia. To think after so many years I'd run into you near Piccadilly Circus!"

"Do you live here?" she asked.

"I do." He dropped into a chair. I noticed the mole on his chin, his inquisitive brown eyes. A paisley neck scarf was tucked loosely into his shirt collar. "I'm in Kensington High," he said. "Before that, for years and years, I was in Hampton Heath, and before that, when I was just starting out a cold-water flat in Chelsea." He laughed. "How dull, my addresses. Tell me, what brings you to London, Hiram?"

"I have family in Sudbury."

This man made me suspicious. His shoes looked expensive and he wore an amber pinky ring. Next to him, even with her Italian knit sweater and slim skirt, my mother appeared shy and quaint, almost the same age as I was. I felt like putting my arms around her shoulders, protecting her.

"How did you wind up living in London, Hiram?"

"The name's Ron Cone now, of Cone Advertising, once Cone and Bradley." He grinned. "I guess you could say family reasons too. I married an Englishwoman, Kate Bullock." He held up his palms. "Okay, I know what you're thinking. New name, Brit blue-blood wife. Get this, she's actually half Jewish and ran off to Israel to make *aliyah* and put *me* to shame."

"What are you defending yourself for?" she replied. "I shocked the whole block when I married Warren. They didn't know what an Indian was, they just knew he was a Gentile from the other end of the world, where everyone has a tan."

They laughed. The conversation eased into another place, with another history and way of talking. This mother was softer than the one who talked with Sheila, unafraid to chat with this man from her past. Maybe it was she who was the strong one. She had the courage to leave home.

My mother gestured to me. "This is Meggie. She's fourteen now."

Ron Cone shook my hand as if I were a grown-up. "Beautiful like your mother! You know, young lady, with your looks you could be a model."

"You've said the wrong thing, Hiram. Meggie sneers at clothes and makeup. She's grooming herself to be a frumpy intellectual."

"Ma!"

"It was just a joke."

Ron had inched closer to my mother, twirling a toothpick in his mouth. I wasn't part of this. As their reminiscing dragged on, I knew there was something dangerous in her lingering to talk with Ron. But I also couldn't remember the last time I'd seen my mother so lively and bright-voiced.

"God," he said. "I haven't been back to the old neighborhood in years. My mother shut down her girdle business and moved to Miami, like all the rest. When I take my girls there she makes them gefilte fish and pickled beets and other food they can't stand and tries to teach them Yiddish. She gets to one word— *kopf*—before she falls asleep." They both smiled. "How long has it been, anyway? Are we really that old?"

My mother tossed a lock of hair from her face. She looked too young to me, a woman who didn't take life seriously. "So what happened when your wife made *aliyah*?" she asked.

Ron blinked several times. He seemed surprised by her boldness. "My dear, she certainly didn't return to me."

The room felt charged with hidden signals. I noticed the way my mother angled forward, the slight dip in her shoulders. Ron matched her funny angle. "I have an idea," he said. "Why don't you girls come up and see my new place?"

My mother breathed in sharply and turned to me. "What do you think, Meggie?"

The air was liquid, and the waiters were suspended in mid-motion, as if they too were waiting for my answer. "I guess," I whispered.

Ron Cone lived in a townhouse in a beautiful square with a garden in the center. As he fumbled with the keys in the foyer, my mother and I swapped nervous glances; neither of us seemed sure why we were here. "I run the office out of my home for now," he was saying. It's a great flat. Three floors. My assistant has a separate entrance." On a polished round table sat a vase of yellow and red gladiolus. On the right wall was a brass plaque inscribed "Cone Advertising, 2nd Floor."

Inside we were greeted by one of the brightest, whitest rooms I had ever seen. Sunlight flooded through a plate-glass window. In a far corner, a young woman worked on a stool at a drawing table, boot heels hooked to the rungs. She had straight black hair, and looked a bit Asian. "Hullo, Ron," she greeted him. "Storyboard's almost ready."

He smiled. "Super."

This was Candace, his assistant. She wore a short tartan skirt, with a heavy-link gold chain belt hanging in a loop from her narrow hips. A matching tartan beret hung from a hook on the wall. It made me dizzy, all the white surfaces, the fashionable Candace.

"Come, girls," Ron said, gently taking my mother by the elbow. "I'll show you around."

He led us up the spiral staircase to his office in the loft above. "Isn't this wonderful!" my mother kept exclaiming, in that same girl's voice. The phone rang three or four times, then clicked off. We took another set of stairs, to a compact living room lined with bookcases, each shelf of which held expensive-looking mementos.

I had never been in a room like this. It was prissy, like a woman's, but I sensed something else, a grown man who enjoyed beautiful things, surfaces. A look of appreciation showed in Ron's eyes when they fell on my mother turning in the center of the room, admiring her surroundings. How different he was from my own father, who retreated to his abstract space. Ron went behind a padded vinyl bar and made my mother a gin and tonic and poured a glass of cranberry juice for me.

"So tell me how you wound up marrying an Indian," Ron said. "It sounds far better than my story."

My mother relaxed, sipping her gin. "It was very exciting. At first. We met at Columbia, where he was a student and I was working as a secretary."

My mother's voice carried a distant tone I'd never detected. That chapter was over, and we'd become characters in another, which she now leafed through with pained amusement. "I thought he was the most brilliant and exotic man I'd ever met. His talk—" She smiled. "He's from the West Indies, you know. And can they talk."

Ron smiled back. "I see more and more of them here in London, yes."

My mother and I both heard it—the strangeness of her story, the whiff of betrayal.

"And you fell madly in love?"

Gazing into the bottom of her glass, she said, "Yes, very much so. And honestly, Hiram—I mean Ron—he really is quite brilliant. A bit disorganized, but all he's read!" This last phrase she emphasized, as if the number of books was offered in competition with Ron's delicate vases and framed prints. She gulped down her drink too fast and splashed a little on her sweater.

Unwilling to listen anymore, I wandered downstairs. Candace was gone. I could hear my mother and Ron as I went into the bathroom with my packages. There I undressed, my reflection flashing in the mirrors that covered the walls. I stood on the toilet seat and checked my arms and legs to see if Sheila's coconut-lemon oiling had changed my skin color. When I lifted my breasts in my palms I noticed that they creased at the top. I kissed the mirror, left an oval of fog on the glass. Then I brushed my nipples with the back of my hand, and waited to feel something. A delicious shiver crept down my spine, as had happened when I was with Peter.

I put on one of my new outfits, a green cardigan and beige skirt. I experimented with my glasses. When they were on, I winced at the dozens of Meggies who stared back at me. The cardigans gave their skins an olive tint. I took off my glasses. This seemed worse. The faces blurred, the colors went muddy. I could hear voices run together in my mind. *There are so many byways,* my father warned. *You have to take a stand,* Peter insisted.

As I tiptoed up the stairs, my mother was still talking about my father, in words that weren't spoken in our house, no longer sweet and amusing. Her voice was close to the sound of crying.

Neither of them saw me as I crouched on the stairs. My mother and Ron sat close together, his arm across the back of the sofa. Because his head was tipped forward, I couldn't see the expression on his face. The table lamp showed my mother's makeup, blue eye shadow, the crimson pencil that lined her lips. Ron asked about what was going on between her and my father. My mother's feet crossed at the ankles; then came a wistful exhale of words: "It isn't what I thought it would be like, no. Actually, it's much better. For all of us. I've learned this over the years, the hard way. I stay out of his hair. This way he won't get distracted. I don't expect more than I get."

When Ron put his hand to my mother's cheek, it wasn't only them I saw, but all the scenes I'd imagined taking place behind my parents' bedroom door. I slipped my glasses off and saw her arms raised above her head, her nightgown twisted over her hips like a ghost of another body, with urgencies of its own.

I put my glasses back on. They had both stood. Ron was hugging my mother. The back of her sweater was pushed up; I could see the soft white fold of her waist. She was no longer the dreamy mother whose belts hung loose over her hipbones; who came to England to live another life, to pretend there was a better one to be found here. Now she was a middle-aged woman with an absent husband. Ron Cone's hands were spread across her shoulder blades. A sadness flooded through me, a sharp, old ache, for I had never seen my father hold my mother like this.

"Megan?" I heard my mother call as I stole downstairs and collected my packages. "Are you all right?"

When I spoke, I found my throat was sore, as if I had been screaming for a long time. "I'm fine, Mom. I'm just going to get some fresh air."

Outside I walked fast. A few minutes later I found the tube station and boarded the train. Once I reached Sudbury, I started to run. Shop windows flowed like a wet paintbox, with horrid browns and greens. By the time I reached our gate, tears streaked down my cheeks. I raced into the darkened house and up the stairs to the bedroom where my father worked.

My father's books, his accordion files were nowhere to be seen. On the desk lay the application, filled out, and a manila envelope. Hearing a noise behind me, I turned.

My father stood in the doorway. He looked neater than at any other time I'd seen him this summer. His hair had been trimmed, its waves tight against his head. He wore a fresh shirt and pressed trousers. We looked at each other in silence.

"You finished the application," I said.

"You were away." He nodded at the desk. "I called Arun and he's going to write a recommendation." He noticed the packages I had thrown on the bed. "Where's your mother?"

I hesitated. "She's having dinner with an old friend."

He came near, put both hands on my shoulders, pulled me close. "And you, my darling?"

I could feel the slow draw of his breaths against my hair. I had never felt so calm, so sure of our balance together, perfect as two matching weights. "Dear Meggie," he said. "Just remember. You drink too much family sweetness and you can't see ahead of you. That's why you have to choose."

There are some things you can do, for the knowledge is there, waiting to be drawn out. After my father went downstairs, I sat on the bed for a long time and let my mind follow its own hidden pull. The dark gathered around, gained mass. The dresser, with its carved drawers, asserted its solidness. The wood box glowed a smooth red, and Aunt Edith's letters were stacked neatly beside it. I dove into a still blackness where I could see only myself shining back.

I got up, opened the box, stroked its velvet lining. I smoothed each of the letters into a blue square and pushed it under the velvet folds. My bangles glinted in fiery circles from my arm. I slipped them off, let their cool weight rest in my palms. I pressed them on top of the letters like a seal, and the box shut with a musical clink.

At the desk, I read my father's application. *I am reaching the end of my inquiry,* it began. In the column for accommodations, I checked "Two rooms," then tucked the pages into their envelope. From the drawer I took a fresh pad of paper and a pen, and wrote.

Dear Edith,

Thank you for your letters. It's been a very difficult summer for us. I'm afraid Warren can't send anything now. He has very important work and can't be disturbed. Love to all.

Sonia

As I signed my mother's name, I was seized with a clear and terrible vision. I could see down to Guyana, where the old family house had come unmoored. Inside, Aunt Edith started up in her bed and pounded her breasts; her spectacles flashed in rage. Torn letters stirred near her feet. Wind rattled the panes. My grandfather came rolling through my father's boardinghouse window, and fell upon my father, dug his knuckles into his neck. Next came Uncle Joseph, a corkscrew of wind himself. He and my father twisted across the floor.

Once I had sealed the envelope, my vision ebbed. The room went still. None of them could hurt us, I told myself, as my plan stitched into neat rows. Next summer I would follow my father to Cambridge and help him finish his book. When he was done, he would gather his papers in his accordion folders and lock them away for the rest of time. He would live with us, before my mother disappeared, with her secret smiles. He would pack away the sad stories of the home left behind. I would lead him upward, to the truth, and back down again, home.

The philosopher king is always leaving. As his plane banks in a far-off land, he sees the dazzling reefs of lights below and thinks he has arrived in heaven. Instead he has come to a place that baffles him, with click-switch lights and subway turnstiles. Everything whirls and shuttles at a breathless speed. He longs for the slow, lazy rhythm of a country road, the magnificent sky overhead, a strange light falling down.

The philosopher king is always walking. Year after year he travels, searching for this mysterious light. From each place he visits he takes a small burning star that he carries in his pocket, as a reminder of his journey. Eventually, the king comes to live on a bench at the top of a hill, where he can contemplate the light he has yet to discover.

The philosopher king is always sitting on his bench. He gathers the streaming moonlight into his palm, turns it upside down, squeezes it into pellets or strokes it into long strands. Every night it spills out, and he wakes with only the cooled stars in his pockets.

After many years, the philosopher king grows very dis-couraged. He flings the stars angrily into the dark. "It's no use!" he cries. "I can't understand anything! My life is a waste."

To his amazement, the bits of broken stars fall into a dazzling pattern. A head, two arms, two legs. Before him appears a vision of a girl. First she flows like water around his eyes. Then she turns solid, clear and sharp as ice. Her eyes shine, black and determined as his. She has a stubborn chin, like his sister's. She wears tight jeans and a halter top, which embarrass him.

She holds her arms out. "Come, Father, I can help you find what you're looking for."

"I can't. I'm a failure."

"That's not true. Remember Yagnavalkya in the Upanishads. For every question you ask, I will build a wheel and another wheel, and finally we will have a chariot to take us to find this light."

"How many states are there for man?" the philosopher king asks.

"Two."

Two wheels, rimmed with gold leaf, miraculously appear and begin spinning under them. "The state in this world, and the state in the next."

"There's another state. And what do you think that state is like?"

The girl is not sure how to answer. She doesn't recall any multiple-choice questions about the third state on the standardized tests at school. Then she remembers that when she can't fall asleep at night she often imagines a tunnel under her bed that burrows under the ocean floor, leading to her aunts in a distant place, who oil and plait her hair and feed her chunks of sweet fruit. Another tunnel shoots straight across the Atlantic to her cousin's bedroom in England, where the two of them prance around and act out their favorite TV shows.

"There's also a third state, between these two, which is like a dream." At these words, another two wheels appear and turn in rhythm, shedding rainbow-hued flakes.

"And what do we experience in this dream?"

"In the dream state, no real chariots or horses or roads or real ponds or rivers or lakes exist. No buses or highways or department stores or movie theaters. A light burns inside you, and you're the one who creates the chariot and horses and roads and lakes."

As the girl gives her answer, a chariot springs up around them. Its dashboard flashes, its seats are made of Naugahyde, its silver wheel hubs dance with sparks. A team of horses, their manes silken tassels, strain forward. A soft, sure wind presses at their backs. They ascend into the sky. The chariot streaks faster and faster, past the spun frost of stars, toward the blazing sun.

The girl is so proud she doesn't notice time lurch forward. The philosopher king starts to age. His hair turns gray, his muscles sag. The surer the girl's course, the more he sinks into a shadow. The chariot picks up speed, tipping from side to side, and the sun grows too hot. The philosopher king feels his head will burst into flames.

"Please, stop! I can't bear it any longer!" He jumps from the chariot, bleeding a tail of embers.

Terrified, the girl brakes to a halt. At first she is heartbroken, left alone in her empty chariot, the philosopher king disappeared into the cold night sky. Then, to her amazement, she sees he isn't really gone. His spirit lights up the entire sky, the land below, the rivers and seas and airports and movie theaters, illuminating a kingdom that is now hers to enter.

Fire

I loved my father's boardinghouse, a gray stone building with white shutters, the only dab of color red begonias in the window boxes. His room was furnished simply—a twin bed he kept stripped down, folded blanket and pillow in a rectangle at its foot; an armchair; an empty desk and small bed table. His bag and clothes were arranged in a circle around the room. Even his change was stacked in four columns on a windowsill.

This summer I stayed in Sudbury for two weeks, then took the train to join my father in Cambridge. Now that I was fifteen, my mother had given up on our being together as a family. She was more mysterious than ever. At my aunt and uncle's house the phone rang at odd hours, calls for her; she would disappear, I guessed to the city. Once she was gone for a whole day and returned late at night. My aunt and uncle said nothing.

"This place is marvelous, Meggie," my father told me after we put my luggage in his room and went downstairs. "I have never felt so full of hope."

He had lost weight, and shadows ringed his eyes. A clarity showed in his face, like a rock washed bare after a long rain. Yet something scared me, for he seemed both solid and vaporous at the same time.

"And listen here," he continued. "Arun has arranged a meeting with the philosophy department so I can give a presentation on my book. He says if it's all I promise, this might lead to something else. Maybe a special appointment." He squeezed my arm. "Nila will be coming too."

"Oh, great."

The last time I'd seen Nila, she was dressed for a classical dance concert, her long black hair in a pretty twist above her neck. Her waist was a slim bow shape and her wrists tinkled with thin red glass bangles. I was envious of her and Arun that night as they walked to the car. Her supple back reminded me of the smooth bend of her father's nose, the easy confidence that rippled in his legs. They'd molded themselves to a beautiful purpose, father and daughter, no cracks showing.

"Let me show you the carrel Arun got for me," my father said, and guided me outside.

We took a narrow path along the banks of the River Cam to the library, another gray stone building, with a cobbled courtyard. My father pointed out the neat beds of white mums and blue hydrangeas; the marble steps and heavy oak door; the rounded tower and the worn marble steps that led to the chamber where he worked.

His carrel puzzled me. It was empty but for three spiral notebooks on a shelf. My father gazed outside the window at the quad and rubbed the wire spines. His hands were not the same as I remembered; they jerked and twitched. "This is what I do," he said, and sat down. "Every day I sit right here, exactly like this." He scraped his chair a few inches so that he could sit with his elbows on the desk. Then he spread open one of the notebooks. The pages were blank.

"This way I can see the clock in the right-hand corner and the grass below. I can watch who comes from that corner, over by the west, and who comes through the gate." Smiling, he smoothed down the pages. "It's a perfect view," he added. A moment later he craned forward, squinted through the window, and muttered something. "Leave me be," I thought he said, but with his face turned from me I couldn't be sure.

"Dad?"

Jumping to his feet, he shut the notebook, put it back on the shelf, and returned the chair to its place. He wiped the desktop with his cuff, as if polishing a brass tray. "Come, darling." He cupped my elbow, indicating it was time to leave.

I wanted to open a notebook and touch the cream-white pages, find the quiet watermark of his thoughts. A sound, like handfuls of pins tossed against the window, broke our reverie. Outside it was drizzling, and rain spattered the pane. We went back to the boardinghouse, shielding ourselves from the slanting drops with a folded newspaper. In the foyer, as we shook out our coats, Mrs. Tuttle, the landlady, rushed up to us.

"There you are, Professor Singh! Didn't you say we'd meet up after the train came in, so I could give you the key to your daughter's room?" She had a large, florid face and peevish eyes. Her lipstick was a crooked slash, as if in the middle of putting it on, she'd turned to pay attention to something else.

My father gave a sheepish shrug. "I forgot."

"You are impossible! Always on your own track." I think Mrs. Tuttle saw in me a comrade-in-arms against my father's forgetfulness, for she steered me upstairs and chattered like an old friend. "We got quite a place, a curious lot, they are, staying here," she commented. "There was a Japanese fellow who made me put his mattress on the floor and gave me extra money to buy new linens."

The room she took me to was cozier than my father's. A plump eiderdown covered the bed and a small heater hummed in the tile fireplace. "Now, your father, he's funny, he don't want me going into the room and changing the sheets at all," Mrs. Tuttle told me. "He leaves his bedding in a pile outside his door every few days." She placed a key on the bedside table. "I suppose it's easier that way. I won't move things to the wrong place. So smart and charming, your father is. Everyone loves to hear him talk. Someone like that, they do their bedding a little different, eh?"

She eyed me in a way that I knew meant she expected an explanation. "He's on a deadline," I offered.

After Mrs. Tuttle left, I went to my father's room, where I found him at his desk, a notebook before him.

"It's still early," I said. "Why don't you let me type up your notes?"

Slowly he shut his notebook and turned to me, hands folded.

"Meggie, it's very important that you learn the system we're working under here. This isn't like before. There are no simple answers. This isn't about doing the obvious."

My father's eyes bored through me, to reach a cool, distant point where nothing mattered except this last chapter. And I so wanted to join him there.

"What can I do, then?" I asked.

"You must be fearless enough to do nothing."

"I don't know what you mean."

"That's a start. Admitting what you don't know. Now you must make your mind like a child's, with no expectations."

I returned to my room. As I undressed, I could hear my father move about next door. It was the restless creak of his chair, the padding of slippers as he sat, got up, sat once again. I made out a noise: he was quarreling with someone. His voice went into a thick Caribbean dialect. "I tell you, leave me be, I got work to do!" A burst of angry gibberish, then silence.

I thumped on the wall. "You all right, Dad?"

It took a moment, and then his voice drifted through, guarded and brittle. "Go to bed, Meggie. I'm fine."

Under the sheets, I lay listening for sounds from the other side of the wall. A drumming started on the roof, and rain splattered on the stones below.

Every morning we had a breakfast of poached eggs and white toast in the front room with periwinkle-blue curtains, then took the narrow lane to the library. There I was permitted to sit quietly in a carrel near his and read or sort his old notecards. At one o'clock we ate a light lunch of cheese sandwiches at the pub, then took a brisk stroll around the shops and resumed our places at the library. When the clock tower chimed five, we gathered our belongings and returned to the boardinghouse. Later I would find him at his desk, staring into space.

He and I had no dialogues, no late-night talks. He preferred to spend most of his time at his carrel, barely talking to me. The starkness of his quest entranced me—the clean, boiled light that fell through his dormer windows, his notebooks, which he stored out of sight in the second desk drawer. I knew he was writing, but he kept it from me. I was still undeserving.

Even my father's erratic behavior was a test of my self-discipline. He complained of voices in his mind, how they made it hard for him to think straight. I noticed how easily his face clouded over when he was interrupted. By the second week I confined myself to only a few remarks at breakfast or lunch. I learned to live in silence, except for the sounds on the other side of the wall—more pacing, more talking under his breath. Soon I came to relish this pattern of silence and noise. Each sound was a clue, a trail of stones I followed through moving water.

With each outburst from his room, I grew more certain it was my thoughts he detected. He could hear the angry, wayward patter of my mind. Worse, he could feel my impatience, how my thieving hands longed to dig inside his desk drawer and be done with this chapter, once and for all.

The third week into my stay I dared to ask if I could see a small section of his work. He made a great show of opening his drawer, lifting the notebook from under sheaves of blotter paper. He pointed to an open page. It was completely blank.

I hesitated, sensing a philosophic trick. "There's nothing."

He smiled. "I knew you'd say that. That's what you must

understand. In emptiness there's fullness. We must train our minds to lose the self, to see better and catch the flow of reality." He clapped the notebook shut. "Now Meggie, you must prove to me that you are ready for such a task."

That night I couldn't sleep. Finally I had been given a real purpose! I sat on my bed and tried to make my mind catch reality. Without my glasses, the edges of the bureau spilled into the brass headboard, then blurred into the wavy eiderdown. How could I see these objects without words, hold in my palms a perfect fullness of meaning?

For the next few days I invented my own form of penance and study. I barely ate, and gave myself to the stream of hours. At first it was hard to quell every urge. I tried to imagine myself a Greek ascetic in a gray, rocky landscape. Often I would set myself on a bench outside to test my powers. When a group of boys and girls would go by, I had to press down the warm yearning inside me. I was better than they, I told myself. I had a far greater mission.

I forced myself to stay away from my father's room. Sometimes I walked until late at night, until my knees grew chilled and my feet ached. These moments, when everyone else seemed snug inside the festive square of a window, were my best. A stark gravity came over me. I especially liked to walk along the Backs, protected by the ragged curtain of trees. I saw the most fantastic and minute of things—a bending stem, the veiny inside of a leaf that pulsed under a patch of reflected moon, the burr of an acorn as it swung in the breeze. Everything was enlarged. My stomach rumbled, I grew faint. One blink and, in an instant, the scene evaporated.

Waking one morning, I touched the ridge of my hipbone

and realized I had lost weight. When I opened the armoire, my blouses and skirts shouted their boastful colors. I left the boardinghouse and bought a pair of brown carpenter pants and a blue work shirt. Now I felt swaddled and safe.

At the boardinghouse, I stowed my typewriter under the bed. Sitting before the vanity, I took a pair of scissors and cut my hair. The strands that brushed against my neck soothed, like a mother's touch. I could not say exactly what I was doing. I only knew I must strip myself down, become pale as a vapor, unthreatening, unseen.

"You've done very well, Meggie," my father said to me when I stood before him in my new outfit. "Now you can help me."

I was delighted that we could take our old places and begin. My father sat in the middle of the room, a candle in a brass holder before him on the floor. "If you were to describe light, how would you?" he asked.

"Daddy, we've talked about this a million times," I reminded him.

"Just bear with your old man a moment."

I gave him my answer from many such conversations: "Something that lends shape and color to the material world."

"Very good! And in your mind?"

I paused. What did he mean by that? He rose and started to pace. "Listen here. *Prana* stands for energy, life force. We also know that Brahman is the Self where there is no duality. You remember what I taught you?"

"Prana is the soul of the universe, assuming all forms. It's the light that animates and illuminates all."

"And how do we know prana?"

"It's visible and invisible. It's the shining sun and cloud cover, it's the well and the well's water."

"And how can prana be both?"

"The difference is only in the naming of things."

My father paused and tilted his head. "You're very well trained after all these years. Yet I fear we have given in to the temptation of pat answers. Particles are not the same as energy units. To see through a paradox is much harder than that."

From his pocket he brought out a matchbook. He lit a match and held it over the candle wick. The flame briefly sputtered, then burned steady, shedding a soft glow around us.

He pointed to me. "Why, since the beginning of time, has fire obsessed us?"

"Because it's the most important element?" I suggested.

"Think of it, Meggie. Every culture has a story of someone who wants to steal the power of fire. Remember the gods went in search of Agni, the fire god, but he always hid himself in the water and the trees. When the frogs and the elephants betrayed his hiding place, he bent their tongues backward so they couldn't speak."

He touched the back of my neck and forced me closer to the candle.

"Look. Do we really know what fire is? Is it the sparks flying into the air, or the smoke trailing off?" He passed his finger through the flame. "What's the difference between my flesh and this candlelight?" He nodded to me, to indicate I should do the same.

I hesitated, though I was afraid of failing him. The candle flame reminded me of a tawny stream, soft and undulating. But as I stared longer, its center became solid bone. I understood. I must go inside, where the core was singed to a clean white purity. I put a finger through, and winced at the sharp pinch of heat. "It hurts. That's how you know the difference."

"That's only pain. Pain rests in the mind."

"Not in the body?"

"What is the body, but a conception?" My father rushed across the room, slapping the heel of his hand on his forehead. "Words, words," he said. "Dammit all, there are no words!"

I stood. "Wait, Dad, we can figure this out. We just have to be patient."

He held out a warning hand, to silence me. Then he started to rock, shoes creaking. "Remember, the two of us can solve this. But you must be a good daughter."

When he brushed his lips on my hair, I was so overcome I held tight to his waist. All of a sudden I remembered the party the summer before, the chemical taste of lip gloss, my stomach warm under Peter's fingers. How I ached for someone to touch me again.

With a shudder, my father pulled away, as if he'd heard my thoughts. "Go to sleep now."

I tiptoed to my room and sat on my bed. It was hot where my father had touched my hair. I kept replaying the scene, fists pressed to my temples. Had I held on too long? To scrape away this skin, these foolish thoughts stuffed inside my head!

On the other side of the wall, the voices started up. "Why you put all that bother an' fool talk in my head!" he shouted. Dammit. I shut my eyes and tried to conjure that single candle flame, burning thin and pure. Concentrate, I told myself. Concentrate.

Nila Bannerjee sauntered into the dining room, an embroidered Kashmiri shawl draped across her shoulders. My jealous
eyes cut her up—narrow waist, sleek black hair, bell-shaped
earrings. While our fathers sat at one end of the table to talk
about their work, she asked me bluntly, "Do you have a boyfriend?"

My first thought was to laugh at her. Didn't she notice my
work shirt and short haircut? Next to her, my plainness hurt. I
didn't want to say anything out loud, for it could cheapen my father's and my work. "Sort of," I said.

"I don't. But I'm not worried. I know a lot of guys who will
go with a girl and ruin her but they won't marry her."

"Is that right." I felt another surge of contempt. This was
mere girl's prattle, recited from script. My father had taught me
to speak with care, to test the weight of my meaning, each
phrase laid out like a smooth bead.

"If I don't find a boyfriend by the time I'm twenty-one," she
continued, "I'll let my father find a match for me."

"How would you know he's the right one?" I asked.

She tossed her shawl from her shoulders and folded it over
the back of her chair. I saw her palm, lined like mine with thin
brown creases, her wrists narrow. So we were not that different,
after all. "I'll know. He must be well educated and come from a
good family. It'll work out."

I was furious at the calm that rested behind Nila's eyes. It
seemed so easy for her to leave her father and move on. Again I
almost blurted what I'd been doing here in Cambridge, but was
afraid it would sound odd.

"Come, girls!" Arun called to us. "What kind of visit is this without our beautiful daughters beside us?"

Nila perched on the arm of her father's chair, while I did the same with my father.

"You're absolutely right to use Hindu thought in your analysis," Arun was saying. "You remember the story of Ramakrishnan? How he stared and stared at the image of Kali and saw only her two sides. One fierce, the other like a mother. One day he found release. You've reached your answer, my man."

"You're simplifying," my father objected.

"No, he's not," I said.

The two men looked at me.

"Then how would you move past the particle–wave paradox, Megan?" Arun asked.

I didn't like the sound of his voice, so oily and polished. He didn't particularly care about my answer; he only savored the entertainment we were creating. It was nothing like when my father and I had our private talks and he hung on my every answer.

I shut my eyes and remembered the burning candle. And now there was Nila, who knew exactly who she was, how she would marry. I knew no such thing. Yet I was sure I could put a hand inside the flame, pull out a hidden truth, perfect as a crystal.

"It's like this," I said slowly. "My dad always taught me that we were in between. He's Indian from the West Indies and my mother is not. We live in the States but we come here every summer to be with Uncle Tom and Aunt Inez and George and Timmy. Light is like that. Here and there. In between."

Arun clapped loudly. "A very good analogy, my dear." He

stood and pointed at me. "Your answer, my man, is in this little girl's mind."

I expected to be showered with admiring words from my father. Instead he shifted in his seat, away from me. "On the contrary, Arun," he said dryly. "My daughter has allowed herself to be distracted by the most superficial of metaphors. She has hardly found the answer."

When the Bannerjees got up to go, I was so ashamed and angry I reached for Nila's shawl. I wanted something that would hang easily yet hide me, cover my failure. The fabric ran cool and slippery between my fingers.

"Meggie!" Nila tried to tug the shawl from my grip.

I wouldn't let go. I had to have that shawl, with its mauve and green stitches curled along the hem. There was the softness of the wool, the way it draped on the round of a shoulder, made an elegant line of the arm.

"Meggie!" she repeated.

When my fist opened, I saw that I had torn a corner, and that the stitching was very bad quality, for it unraveled into frayed threads. Nila let out a cry. She swept the shawl up, folded the torn corner under her arm, and flounced out of the room.

"How could you say such nonsense?" My father paced across his room, shirttail over pajama pants. In irritation he kicked an empty tobacco pouch, and it popped up like a deflated balloon. "Nonsense!"

"I was just trying to help," I ventured.

"Instead you've set us back. I thought we'd gone to deeper

levels. Now you must start again. Your answer was too clever, too knowing. You must have a child's mind."

"I'm not a child, Daddy."

He waved an impatient hand. "You remember, as you used to do before. You have to return to true knowledge, not worldly knowledge."

He kept pacing. "Maybe Arun has a point. Maybe this conflict of particle and wave is a kind of illusion." His steps came to an uncertain stop. "Maybe *I'm* the illusion."

I stared at him. My father was falling away from himself. The skin of his cheeks drooped away from the bone. Day and night, all he ate was words, and now they were eating at him.

"I don't understand what's happening. Days go by. I look up and I have no idea what I've been doing. I see my notebooks, but I can't remember anything at all! It's a blankness." He added softly, "I wonder if I've gone too far. I'm afraid I'm becoming the blankness."

I rested my hand on his arm as another tremor seized him. "Dad, you need to sleep."

"You don't get it!" he said. "If I can't figure out what light is, I will lose! I can't be sure about anything! Who *I* am!" He grabbed my hand. "You're here, Meggie! You can help me. You remember, like the old days."

"Okay. Let's start from the candle—"

"No!" he shouted. "I told you, it must be simple. Otherwise the voices, they'll come in. They'll ruin everything!"

"I can make them go." I focused on the dormer window, but I could not make my vision stay. I wanted to leave the room, crawl under the eiderdown on my bed. My thoughts slipped. Stupid book. Enough.

"Don't say that," my father moaned. "Don't ever say that. You're supposed to be helping, but you're muddling my mind!"

He swayed like a too-full bottle and covered his ears with his hands. As I put my arms around him, a strange image came to me. I could see inside his mouth, the bones of his face. He had thrown his weight against me, yet he seemed to weigh nothing at all. I prodded him into his bed, where he collapsed with relief. "You have come for me," he said.

"Hush." I drew the blanket over him.

"Your face is a lie."

"You sleep now."

Outside, rain was coming down hard, and the Cambridge spires sank under a thick wedge of fog. If I tidied up, my father would get better. We would both get better. He began to thrash in the covers. "I don't want to! Don't make me, *please!*"

First I peeled off his sweaty shirt and sponged him down, scooped the musky scent from his armpits, washed the dark whorls of his knuckles. Then I trimmed his nails, swept away the slivers, brittle as insect husks, from the sheets, and ran a pumice stone along the rough edges of his heels. When I was done, I could see him shine from the inside with a thick orange glow, like a copper Buddha.

For hours I soothed his forehead with a damp cloth. I chanted different words for light, the gods of fire, all my father had taught me. I hoped the words might be a hard lozenge of sound, their meaning passing gentle through our minds, calming us to a perfect silence. Be good, I told myself. Make yourself pure as the marrow of a flame.

Daddy! I heard myself cry. *Stay with me!* My lids were heavy. I tried to count the coins on the windowsill, but I was so tired they glittered and spun from my eyes. I called out the simplest of things, the names of his students, the titles on the spines of his books at home. *You are here now,* I told him. *You are here.*

The next morning I woke to find my father dressed, wiping down his desk. His few notebooks were gone. The bedding, his clothes, the columns of coins had also disappeared. He looked the part of the energetic, handsome professor, gray hair combed into an elegant swirl, tweed blazer with elbow patches, wine-colored corduroys.

"Hello, sleepyhead, you ready for a little jaunt?" he asked.

"A jaunt?"

"I thought we might rent one of those punts on the Cam."

"What about your chapter?" I asked.

He gave one last swab with the rag and set it down. "I woke up this morning and everything was clear. I knew my answer." He touched his desk drawer and the handle jiggled. "Done!"

Done? I thought, sinking with disappointment. How could he find the answer, without me? I longed to pull the drawer open, touch the pages myself.

The day was brilliant and clear, the shingle roofs glazed with drying rain. We walked down the lane to Scudamore's landing and rented a punt. I handled the long pole, and enjoyed figuring out how to dip and push into the current.

Once out on the river, my father seemed calm. He took his pipe from his jacket pocket, filled it with tobacco, dipped a match in the bowl. Cottony tufts of smoke bobbed over his head. "How lovely," he remarked. "We should do this more often."

"You were busy, Dad."

He knocked his pipe against the boat, and ashes scattered like dried butterfly wings. "It's all my fault. I've been off in the clouds, forgetting about my little girl here. Now life really begins, Meggie."

I still couldn't believe it. The water's ripples hurt my eyes.

"You've put up with me all these years," he continued. "From now on, it's going to be different. I promise. We can do things, not like before. I'll take you places."

"You don't have to," I assured him.

Of course, I wanted nothing more. I wanted to stay with him, drifting forever, never worrying about his book again. Swans glided by, showed the graceful tuck of their necks; the Cambridge towers stood tall against a polished-nickel sky. We eddied up the River Cam, cutting a lazy course; willows brushed our shoulders as he and I wove our own make-believe story.

We were in a restaurant, a gorgeous, grown-up one with deep plush booths and velvet curtains tied with braided rope. My father called for wine, and our imaginary waiter floated toward us, glasses balanced like two small hearts. My father raised his wineglass in a toast, to us, our real vacation, father and daughter reunited. "Now it's your turn. My work is over," he said.

I felt myself unfold under his admiring gaze; my bare brown arms, my freshly combed hair, chin tipped to meet his feverish eyes. A bright peace lay thick around us, dabbed between the leaves of the trees. I was so lucky to have this father, I thought, as we rounded a bend. No one else could know the secret hollow we curled inside as the sky poured its glittering energy through a pinhole of stories.

He held up his imaginary glass. "To you, Megan. To your brilliant journey into the future."

"Oh, Daddy," I said. "What about you?"

"You don't have to deceive your old man. I know what you want. You want my answer. If I told you, you'd throw it in the water again, wouldn't you?"

Confused, I dug the pole into a spot of bruised water. Noises skimmed past. I glanced up, sure they had slipped through the clouds.

"All children want to steal their parents' passion, isn't that right?" he asked.

Our restaurant evaporated. I saw my father's face from the night before, a mask that fell away from bone. I poled faster and slashed the water, churning up furrows. Then the pole tip caught on a clump of reeds. My palms burned as I pulled, hard. The punt swayed and rocked.

"Megan!" my father protested. "What are you doing, sweetheart?"

The front of the boat thudded against pilings, and our knees bounced on the slatted seats. When I stood, I skidded in the slippery puddles. I grabbed the rope for balance, and calmed myself with throwing it over, tying it to the post and clambering onto the dock. Then I felt my father's hand on the small of my back.

"Darling," he whispered. "You're afraid."

I let him take me in his arms, breathed in his familiar tobacco-and-wool scent. "It's going to be all right," he said. "You go back to the boardinghouse. I'll join you in a little while."

"Don't leave."

"I'll be back very soon. After we can start packing and go home."

"Promise?"

He stroked my hair, which burned hot from the sun. Then

he turned and left. I watched him walk down the road. Sun licked the edges of his sleeves until his silhouette mingled into late-afternoon shadows. Soon he disappeared beneath the trees.

Back at the boardinghouse, when I tried his door, I discovered it unlocked. I sat on his bed, feeling useless. I wandered around, traced his vanished steps. The windowsill was wiped clean, except for one shilling. I touched the hem of the curtain and something banged to the floor. It was the brass candlestick, a stub wedged in the round holder. I found a matchbook, sat in the middle of the room, and lit the wick. For a while I listened to the quiet drip of wax, watched the flame, until my lids grew heavy and I fell asleep.

When I woke, the candle had burned down. The room was filled with a deep blue shadow. The desk drawer gleamed, luscious and plum-colored. Inside, I knew, lay a rich and moist truth. I began to pace, trying to keep my hunger down. I remembered the story of my aunt's raiding the larder years before to soothe her parched heart. My feet made tighter and tighter circles. Unable to stand it anymore, I dashed across the room and seized open the drawer.

Inside there was no manuscript. Just one spiral notebook, its cover clean. I riffled through. Each page was blank, except for the date across the top right-hand corner. I flipped ahead. On the last page, there was one line. *It is time.*

Time for what, I thought, as I ran to my room for a jacket and hurried out of the boardinghouse.

Outside, people were crowding the lane to the library. Some even ran, dodging bicyclists who zigzagged amid them, scraping their bicycle bells. A knot of clouds had gathered over the roofs. Rain again. When I reached the library courtyard, I thought it was a class milling on the cobblestones. No. Those weren't clouds, but sprouting columns of smoke.

The library tower was on fire.

From a third-story window, flames bent, made a deep-crimson funnel. A fireman dangled in a canvas belt, hose braced against his stomach. The sill crumbled and a burning chunk spiraled past his shoulder. The crowd surged forward and nearly reached the library wall, until a shock of heat pushed us back. A boy in a blue sweater jostled against me. "Hullo," he said. "Take a look up there."

I craned my neck, scanned first to the tower, then to the library building. High on its parapet, a figure stood against the iron rail, arms akimbo, hair wild and silver in the smoky air. My father. My father stood on the roof, shouting at the crowd.

"You hear?" a girl behind me said. "It's some Indian professor up there."

"Christ," someone else remarked. "They don't stop a bloke like that, and see what he does."

I wanted to say, "No, you're terribly mistaken, he's doing very important work," but I could not get the words out.

My father leaned over the iron rail, palms up. "Quiet, all of you!" he said. "The lecture is about to begin." Titters of laughter broke out around me as he pointed to the flames spearing smoke.

"Angels of fire!" he shouted. "Have you no idea what I can teach you? Answer this! What are the elements of the universe?"

"Do I get an A if I tell you?" someone asked.

"What's the reading list?"

My father beamed. "You don't know. Heracleitus believed that fire is the root of all things. I have a better answer. I am the Professor of Light! Everyone knows! Dr. Raj knows! The most brilliant minds of this university know! I can see!"

He lapsed into a scolding patois, his voice hoarse. "What you think, you ghost-men shrinkin' fearful on the earth? We here know de truth! What happen when you cut cane down and boil it in de boilin' house? First it's liquid and den it's crystal! We pass from solid to air, from dry to liquid, through all states of being! We have no real form!"

He scooped up an armload of books. "Fools! You don't need dis," he yelled. "*I* can tell you what you need to know!"

The crowd became restless. Someone called, "Damn him! Look what he's doing now—"

Heads tilted as the books tumbled from the roof, pages fluttering. The boy in the blue sweater bent down and opened one. "Bloody hell. He's destroying rare books!"

"Be quiet," I said. "That's my father." The boy looked at me, puzzled. "That's right," I said flatly, and pushed my hand against his chest. "My father. Now move aside."

The scene wafted into a dream; the flames made a pretty fringe over the damp stones; the crowd parted. A handsome curly-haired policeman stepped forward and touched my sleeve. I gave him a radiant smile. He understood how powerful I was, the thread that connected me to my father, up there. My vision blurred as I sailed past the parade of faces. White plastic rope snapped at my waist, metal doors clanged open. A set of stairs rose before me. I climbed one set and another with the policeman, until we reached an iron ladder that led to a square of drizzly sky. "There you go, luv, I'm right behind you," he told me.

His arm felt solid. "See if you can't give him a talking-to. We'll bring him down that way."

I nodded, edging closer to the wall. Down below, the faces looked ruddy and cheerful in the fire's glow. On the ledge, my father held both arms wide. "All is fire," he bellowed. "All is illusion!"

"Speak for yourself!" someone piped up.

"You laugh!" he admonished. "You have no idea, you Englishmen, all of you are also burning!"

On unsteady knees I climbed onto the ledge. Through the ribbons of heat, faces wavered, in and out. I called to my father softly until he turned around. His face brightened. "Come, my darling!"

I was horrified, yet a tremor of excitement shot through me as I was pulled nearer to the voice I knew so well, its wild, erratic questions. This was my test. Yes. My mind sped into a corridor, one thought shuttled into another. Now. Go inside the light. Walk right through the core of fire, reach the other side.

A woman's shriek pierced the air. The curly-haired policeman leaped up, made quick, panicked motions to me to stop. I flashed him a sure smile. They didn't understand. They didn't see how the fire was opening to me like a body, showing its membranes of color, blue veins underneath. My father knew. "Go on," my father urged. First one step, then another.

A huge wall of orange flame spread before me. It was beautiful, wide as a chrysalis, shot through with yellow streaks. A blast of heat cinched tight around my face. My eyes streamed; I began to cough. I didn't care. I had only to step inside, where white-hot solid melted into translucent wave. One more step and my father would finally see. I would become a floating strand, burn into clouds of light-dust.

A skinny flame leaped out, sliced me across the cheek. Stunned, I touched my chin. My face burst with scalding pain. I could hear a cold, dry voice cut through the roar. My uncle, pulling me back. *It's a balance,* I heard him say. *Always a balance.*

"Don't stop!" my father yelled. "Keep going!"

The next thing I knew, I had sunk to the ledge, a warm wetness on my hands.

"What are you doing?" my father shouted.

"I'm hurt," I gasped.

The policeman uncoiled from his crouch and pressed a finger to his lips. I gave my return nod. Two others stole up from behind. The first policeman grabbed my father's shoulders. Swiftly the others surrounded him, dragged him down. I listened to the scuffle of boots, the hard thump of my father's body as it fell to tar paper.

I don't know how long I stayed there, hunched on the ledge. I could hear the crackle of things burning, a damp wind on my face. Something dropped across my shoulders. It was a fireman's raincoat, slick and rubbery-smelling.

Slowly I made my way to my father and kneeled before him. He lifted a hand, rubbing ash on my cheek. "Oh, my darling," he said. "How I dreamed for you. Joseph says you're the best of all of us." Then he sank against a fireman, eyes blank. I tried to shake him, but he said no more.

The policeman touched my shoulder. "We should get him out."

A moment later clouds broke and rain came slanting down.

An odor, like burning hair, hung everywhere. I followed as my father was carried down the stairs, through a room where firemen dragged fat hoses across soiled rugs. Two workmen were trying to cover the windows, but rain pelted through the shattered panes; black plastic billowed like funeral drapes. Someone brushed my head. Then I realized: It was hundreds of tiny ashes pouring through a hole in the wall.

Once there was a girl in Guyana who was descended from Rajput royalty. Because her father thought her very special, he didn't want her to leave and kept her in a box. Every month he sent her floating down the river so she could feel that she had gone somewhere.

But the father was very clever. He knew he couldn't leave his daughter in a little box forever. When she cried for all she could not see, he built her a bigger box, the inside lid traced with the rivers of Guyana. When that wasn't good enough, he made yet another box. This one was large enough to show all of South America and the Caribbean islands.

The princess wasn't satisfied. "I need to see more of the world, Father," she complained, and he built her an even greater

box, which held the Atlantic and Indian oceans, and all the
continents. Now the princess was able to travel the world over.
She danced from the boot of Florida to New York, skated around
the looping highways of Queens, played hopscotch on the red
roofs of English rowhouses.

Still this girl was not happy. "My hands wish to touch the
stars, Father, and my arms want to embrace the sun."

Now the father built the best box ever. The lid was studded
with diamonds that spread into a map of the entire universe.
"This is real knowledge," he told her. "You need nothing else
now."

The princess felt very lucky, for she could lie in the velvet
bedding and wander very far, discover everything that was
possible, yet she was always protected by her father and his
jeweled box.

One night, when the stars glittered sharp as knives, a boy
caught the floating box with his fishing net and tugged it to
shore. Curious to know what was inside, he pried the lid open. To
his astonishment, he found a beautiful girl. Her arms and legs
were withered and cramped like walnut pieces in their shell, her
eyes were dim and withdrawn.

He took her by the arm and led her to land. For the first
time in ages, the princess's feet walked on real ground and her
eyes took in real sky. Her limbs trembled and shook with these
new sensations. They walked and walked, and the princess
wished the night would go on forever.

The father, waiting for the box to return, grew very angry.
He burned cane for torches and lit up the fields. Finally he saw
his daughter's head bounce in the tall cane as she skipped hand
in hand with the boy. The father's voice thundered, "How dare

you!" At her father's wrath, the girl felt her knees wobble. Her ankles grew weak. Her shoulders hunched as if she was trying to squeeze herself back into her box.

By the time the father caught up with her, the princess was small like a walnut again. He lifted her from the grass, kissed her cold brow, and gently laid her back inside her special box. Then he nailed the lid shut and sent her down the river.

They say that when the moon rises high over the cane fields, you can hear the sound of the Rajput princess in her box, going up and down the rivers, calling out for the sights she can never see, and weeping for the father who betrayed her.

Flight

A month after my father tried to burn down the library, he was released from the hospital and sent to live with us in Sudbury. The family made room for him, as my aunts in Guyana made room for my uncle Joseph. Every day my father woke and put on trousers and clean shirt and cardigan, as he used to dress for classes. He read the newspaper front to back and, if the weather permitted, sat in a canvas chair in the garden, smoking his pipe. He did not say a word.

A deep peace came over him, his face was a carved teak mask. Sometimes his fingers drummed the narrow armrests of his chair. For simple treats, such as an oval of custard, his face opened with hunger. Once he had eaten it, he folded shut again, and disappeared into a mute, blank hole.

Underneath the house spread a damp crater of sadness. We walked in circles around one another, afraid to lift our heads to look through the windows and see what lay beyond. A shade had been pulled down inside me.

Afternoons, my uncle and I gardened together. The August sun shone weak on our backs; a slight nip edged the air. I grew easily bored with the endless trimming and tweaking, the piles of dead leaves at our knees after hours of work. It pained me to come to such a small end. The only hint of what had happened was a thin scar, where the fire had licked my chin. I often touched it, to reassure myself that what had happened on the library roof was not a dream. I had almost walked inside the flame, become light.

It was Aunt Inez's fingers I felt each night as she smoothed the sheets and put the hot-water bottle under the eiderdown. Her touch was simple and strong. She, like her sisters, knew how to survive through silence. She didn't want to hear about what had happened in Cambridge. She wanted only to soothe me back into the family.

"Darling, don't be so glum. You know our boys," she said one night. "Always letting the spirit get to them." Then she told a story of a greedy boy who felt his mother did not feed him enough.

"After school let out, this boy used to take a cast net and walk by the back dam. He go to the black water and catch some of that sweet hassa fish your father and I love. Every day he steal the fish from the lake. This boy get so greedy that one day a fish stick in his throat and he stop talking altogether.

"Months go by and this boy still can't talk. He miss out on

everything. He can't give his answers at school or shout to his friends during the cricket games. One day his mother get mad. She drag him back down to the lake. 'There you go!' she says. 'You want fish so much, you go and swim with the rest of them!' Then she pushed her son's head underwater. That poor boy think he going to die. All around him is dark and more dark. All of a sudden the fish come wrigglin' out his mouth, eager to be with the rest of his kin. And when that boy come up for air, you can bet he talk a silver streak after that!"

She stroked my hair and stood. "You wait, Meggie. Is the same with your father."

I laughed at my aunt's story, but no fish ever swam out of my father's mouth. The only change was in my mother, who grew more beautiful with each passing day. Hers was a sad beauty, like that of a frightened girl who had gotten more than she bargained for. She woke up first and prepared my father's breakfast tray. Later, after lunch, she would leave the house. She would return to us several hours later, cheeks flushed, and go straight to bed.

One night she came into my room and stood over my bed. She wore a nightgown I'd never seen before, with spaghetti straps. The silk clung to her hips like a wet skin, gleamed silver in the dark. A puff of cotton-candy pink showed in her hands. It was a stuffed bear, which she pushed into my face. "There's a carnival over by Horsendon Hill," she said, and got into bed with me. She smelled of perfume and sweat; the bear reeked of sawdust.

"Ma, what are you doing?" I asked.

I saw her shoulders quake. Her skin was a paler shade of

the bear's fur, dusted with freckles. "I can't sleep in there." She nodded toward the bedroom that was hers and my father's. "I just can't."

She slept and her breaths were short and shallow. If I could take her into my own arms, I believed, she would turn to bits of lint. In the morning, when I woke, she was gone; the teddy bear was propped on the pillow.

The next day she did not go out until evening. I decided to follow her as she crossed the street and hurried toward Horsendon Woods. She wore a quilted hunter-green jacket over a cream-colored dress, and moved quickly, bent at the waist. A breeze seemed to push the bottom of her heels and lift her through the air.

We headed down the dirt path, with me several paces behind, hidden in the shadows of the trees. Past a stand of birch trees lay the fair, which stretched from the top ridge of the hill, where the bench was, down the slope, to the flat expanse below. It was funny to see the field where George and I used to lie dreamily in the flattened weeds now crowded with canvas booths that clanged and flashed with yellow- and pink-lit games. At the farthest end stood the Ferris wheel, its center a glowing eye of ruby bulbs. I picked my way through the crowds, eyes on my mother's green coat. A man with a double-breasted blazer stepped from the side of a booth, and led her to a counter that sold mulled wine and beer.

It was Ron Cone.

My mother leaned against the bar, narrow hips angled out, and threw back her head, showing the length of her neck as she drained her cup. Ron wiped something from her mouth with his index finger. They were talking, but I could not hear the words. I waited a few minutes, then inched along the bar, listening.

Her voice rolled in wet, sloppy waves. "If you only knew how absentminded Warren was," she burbled. "Coming home from school, he'd drive around and around Kissena Boulevard because he'd forgotten where we lived! Finally I'd spot our car going by, and I'd run outside. I'd have to wave a dishrag to flag him down." She hiccuped. "Can you believe it—a dishrag!"

She went on, tossing out bitter words, words meant to lengthen the distance between her and my father. I remembered the story of the ribbon turning to blood as she and I flew from Guyana, only now it was I who was hurting.

Ron pushed another cup into my mother's hand. She drank gratefully, the hues from the arcades splashed across her shoulders.

My movements were slow and liquid as I went up the steps and knocked her drink from her hand. "You can't do that!" I shouted.

The cup fell, strawberry-colored drink spilling on the unpainted wood. She twisted around, her eyes unfocused. "Wha-a?" She blanched. "Oh my goodness. Meggie."

"That story," I said. "It isn't funny. Why do you have to talk about Daddy that way?"

Ron stepped forward, looking concerned. "Meggie—"

"Shut up," I said. "Just shut up."

My mother tried to touch my arm, but I yanked away. "Darling, it's just talk to make me feel better."

"No! You're talking like he's gone!" I turned on my heel and ran into the crowd. I kept running, and the carnival colors and my mother's shouts dissolved behind. Then I stopped. I pressed my fingers to my burning lids and dropped to my knees. I wanted to cry, I wanted to bury myself in the damp moss, I wished them both dead.

Later, in my room, I heard footsteps on the stairs, and then a soft, insistent knock as my mother called to me. She rattled the knob, but I had locked the door. Quickly I undressed and crawled under the covers. "Talk to me," she said. I shut off the light. After a few minutes she went away.

By the time I woke the next morning, Sheila had returned to us; her two green suitcases sat like manicured shrubs in the downstairs hall. "All right, then." She clapped her hands to my mother and me. "It's time to get on with the real business." She flung open the curtains in the parlor and told us to fetch my father's belongings from upstairs, declaring it was too depressing to work up there.

"Thank goodness you're here," my mother said with a sigh. "I didn't know where to begin."

In the parlor that afternoon, I watched as she and my mother worked like soldiers connected by secret signals, moving the piles and boxes on the floor. Then my mother sat, notebook propped against her knees, while Sheila called out: "Bank accounts, medical insurance. Telephone numbers and addresses of people in the department." My mother's pen paused over the page. Sheila continued. "A letter to the dean, but don't say too much. Make it sound like he'll be back in a semester or two. Say he's on a rest cure."

"But the doctors say there's no guarantee."

"Forget that. They're not going to ask to see some doctor's report from little old Cambridge." She dropped a book into a box. "Professors take sabbaticals all the time. It's expected that they go off their rocker every once in a while. It makes them more charming. And you must admit, dear, he did do it in style."

The room went quiet. "Sometimes I get so overwhelmed," my mother said in a small voice. She handed Sheila a sheet of paper covered with her cramped handwriting.

"You can't do that!" I yelled.

Sheila let the paper drop to the floor. I shrank against a wall. My mother nodded to Sheila. "Will you leave us alone? Megan and I need to talk."

We sat opposite each other, my mother's hands tight on her lap. "You keep running away from me, Meggie."

"You're the one that's running away."

"Is that what you think?"

I did not answer. My mother crossed to the bay window and touched a curtain. Despite myself, I softened. How many times had I seen her stand by a window, stare out at the street as she waited for my father to return home from his work, to return to her for good?

"I thought you would understand," she said. "You know how it's been for me. In this family, to be a wife is to become like a sister. That's the old way. That's how your father was raised."

I pointed to a cardboard box, its flaps still open. "But how can you get rid of him like this?"

"Don't you see what's going on here? It's like what happened with Joseph. Everyone is gathering around him as if it was normal and it's our duty. I'm dying in this house, Meggie. I can feel the coffin shutting on me."

My mother returned to her chair and stared at her feet. Her

ankles looked too thin for her shoes. Her tailored suit, with its bulky shoulder pads, sat heavy on her frame. She looked like a girl playing dress-up.

"Do you love Ron Cone?"

There was a long pause. "I love the way he loves me," she replied. "He delights in my hands, in the way I look, the littlest things. You have no idea what it's like. It's almost a drug, this feeling."

"Do you love him more than Daddy?"

"Meggie, I would do anything for your father. I *did* do everything for him. Still he doesn't want me. He wants something that is beyond all of us."

"But he's your husband!" I cried.

She raised her hand; for an instant I thought she might hit me. "You stupid, stupid girl," she said softly.

In two strides she was across the room, and she kneeled before me, clutching my sleeve. I wanted to disappear into the folds of the chair.

"I have to breathe, Meggie. You do too. You can't stay trapped like this. You'll die inside. You have to find a way out."

My cheek hurt, from trying to keep a stone-cold face. Inside, though, I was stunned by what she'd said. A breeze blew through the curtains. I could not move as my mother gathered her notebook and walked out of the room.

When my aunt brought the hot-water bottle that night, I pushed her hand away. "My mother——" I stopped. "They're giving up on him."

"Your mother knows what she's doing," she said crisply. Her lashes were spiky and wet.

"What about the story of the fish in the boy's mouth?" I asked.

Aunt Inez sat on the edge of the bed, and in the dim room, I saw her broad back. "Listen to me, Meggie. A long time ago, your father made a promise to take care of us. That way he could leave and not fall to the jumbee curse. But he couldn't hold fast and move on at the same time. He couldn't keep both inside him."

I shut my eyes and was again drifting along the River Cam; the water danced with silvery whirlpools. I wanted only to stay in that boat, a golden light streaming around us, father and daughter, forever joined.

My aunt put a firm hand on my face. "Darlin', it's time to give him up. You got to shout out his name. Otherwise you going to carry the jumbee curse too."

She held her hand there a long time, as if trying to press this urgent thought inside my cheek. I felt every inch of her; her warm palm, her solid bulk that bent the mattress down, her sure faith all these years. *No,* I thought, shrinking from her touch. *I can't call out his name. I can't give him up.*

After she left, I lay curled in my bed, the pink teddy bear beside me. My mother, I knew, had not come home yet. *You got to shout out his name.* She was wrong. My father could talk. It was a joke. A philosophy trick. Any minute now his laughter would splash through the wall.

Then I heard it. The creak of a wooden chair, rustling paper. Mutters. Quiet. The air went still. The air seemed to drum in my ears. I jumped out of bed, went into the hall, and tapped on their door. "Daddy?"

No answer.

"Dad, it's Megan. I'm coming in now."

I turned the knob. Inside, the curtains were drawn shut. I switched on a lamp. A tray with a half-eaten slice of toast and a juice glass sat on a table next to the bed, a teacup on the windowsill. The bed was empty.

He was sitting in a chair, staring straight at me. First I saw the crocheted blanket over his knees, fringes hanging over his thighs, a pouch of a stomach. With his cardigan sleeves bunched at the elbows, he looked as if he might be in the middle of hectic office hours.

His eyebrows were bushy tufts that nearly hid his eyes. I knew those eyes. They were bright and sharp, took everything in, understood all. A weakness showed around his mouth, though, and his lips spread in a loose smile. When he lifted his chin to look at me, he began to shake.

"It's okay, Dad."

The blanket wriggled through his fingers; his knees, now exposed, knocked together.

"I heard you."

His mouth opened once, twice. No sound dropped out.

I advanced, then stopped when I saw his left hand reach for the teacup on the sill. We seemed to taste our silence, waiting. Words dashed through my mind. "Listen to me," I told him. "I heard you talk, okay? I heard you."

My father grabbed the teacup by its handle, swung it over his head, and drove the cup, hard, against the wall. It shattered behind my head. I took another step closer. The saucer whizzed by my ear; another splintering noise. My father's mouth curled into a grin, like that of a boy who has won a schoolyard showdown.

"What's going on?" my aunt called out. "Megan, is that you?"

"Yes, it's me, Auntie. It's nothing. I dropped the clock."

I didn't stop. With both hands I cradled his face. The skin of his cheeks was soft, without muscle. "You talked, when no one was around," I went on. His eyes stared blankly into mine. "Talk to me," I begged. "I know you can." I pressed my fingers into his flesh. "I am going to make you, do you hear me? Now *talk.*"

His jaw was clenched. Tears ran from his eyes. I kept my voice a low, fierce whisper. "You can't do this. You're not Uncle Joseph. You're a professor. We can pack up and go home, the way we always do. You can teach, you just have to try."

My nails dug into his cheeks, and I could feel his whole body shudder. "Listen to me. We can write the last chapter together. We can go to the bench, I'll ask the questions—"

I leaned over him in a menacing arch. My hands squeezed, hard. A gurgling bubbled up from his throat. He did not open his mouth. With one hand I tugged his chin down. I could feel the tense resistance against my palm; his lips parted and I saw the speckled pink roof of his mouth. His teeth were yellow, his lips parched. My other hand kneaded his cheekbones, to press them into the shape of sound. "One word! That's all! Give me one word!"

His face was shiny-wet with tears.

Lunging toward the armoire, I tore open the doors. My fingers grabbed suit shoulders, silk blouses, pleated skirts. I reached for more; shoe boxes, vinyl bags, and books fell to my feet. I picked a book up and flipped it open. "What are you so afraid of?

A book? How can that spook you? It's just printed words, it's nothing." I nudged the open volume into his hands. "Read!"

I smacked my palm at the back of his head and pushed. His nose was inches from the page. He pushed back, but I stayed firm. "Tell me what it says!" A thread of spittle dripped from the corner of his mouth. Great mute sobs wheezed from his chest. *This is your father*, a voice inside me protested. It was too late. I pinched the soft pouch of his neck, felt its startled pulse, then thrust his forehead into the open book. "Read!"

His lips quivered, and his eyes flicked back and forth. When a hoarseness scraped in his throat, a triumphant fire started up in me. It was working, I thought. He's trying to read!

The book tumbled free, grazed my thigh, and dropped to the floor, and I let go my grip.

A moment later, my father sprang from his chair, stumbled over me, and flew out of the room. I made it to the landing in time to catch sight of his red robe as he bolted through the front door.

Quickly I put on my shoes and hurried outside. He was headed down the road. "Daddy, where are you going?" I called. Behind me I could hear a commotion in the house; I turned to see lights blinking on.

I began to run, my eyes on the small flame of a robe as it disappeared into Horsendon Woods. Once inside, I lost my way. I thought I was on the main path, veered to the right, retraced my steps, unable to find the old places I knew so well. It was all fumbling darkness. A bristly animal swerved into me, and I fell back to stare at a bush. Ahead I saw my father streak through an opening in the trees.

"Stop it, now!"

The black lid of sky did not open. The trees loomed thin and tall. "Daddy!" I called again, and rushed on into the empty fairgrounds.

He rounded the ticket booth, disappeared behind the towering shadow of the Ferris wheel, and began climbing the hill. He was headed to the old concrete bench.

"Daddy!"

By the time I reached him, he had hoisted himself onto the bench. I scrambled up, crushed myself to his sweaty chest; his heartbeat fluttered against my cheek.

"I'm sorry," I wept. "I tried to help you. You've got it all wrong. I wanted to help you. Tell me anything. Please. Just talk to me. Don't go away."

A shout broke out. Below, a glimmering chain of flashlight beams moved jerkily along the hill ridge. George sprinted toward us, while Uncle Tom and Aunt Inez came up fast behind.

"He talked!" I told them as they came nearer.

"Megan, your dad isn't well," Uncle Tom said.

"But I heard him!"

My uncle put a hand on my arm. "Megan. Stop it. Look."

My father stood on the bench, arms spread wide, as if trying to hug the tents below. His robe blew at his ankles. He swayed at the edge, and jumped, then tumbled to the ground. Before George could reach him, he had gotten to his feet and mounted the bench.

We watched as he craned his neck; his mouth opened and shut. He was trying to talk! Aunt Inez's eyes followed the silent movement of his lips. The drop was only a few feet, but he hurled himself into the air. A moment later, he fell with a moist thump to the grass. We couldn't stop him, for he had clambered to the seat again.

This time Aunt Inez and my cousin were fast enough. George grabbed his left arm, my aunt clasped a leg. My father struck him across the face, and George staggered backward. "Meggie, help us!" my aunt whimpered. I did not move.

Uncle Tom came from behind, a blanket held between outstretched hands. The blanket seemed airborne, a flash of gray-blue. Then it swallowed my father into its folds. His arms thrashed, but he was tangled too deep. George tackled him from the front; my aunt held his knees as he was dragged from the bench. He was hurt; I saw blood on his chin.

They pinned him to the ground. His legs twitched as he rocked from side to side, moaning. There was a sudden sharp slap. My uncle was hitting my father. Once again. My father went still. Aunt Inez stroked his hair. "It's all right now, Warren. We'll go home now, all right, brother? You have a good sleep now, you forget all this."

He lay on one side, knees at his chest. An old man, curled into himself, needing a good bath and a tuck into bed. Mouth shut. Silent.

"No!" My cry bounced off the empty booths.

My hands touched grass, dirt, the sharp tip of a stone. I flung it to the ground. "He has to talk!" I threw another stone, which cracked against the concrete. With one more stone I pounded at the bench, each hit a current through my arm. The bench was less solid than I remembered, pitted with ruts and holes. "It's all in here," I said. "Every night we came here and he talked and talked—"

A corner of the bench broke loose. Small chunks of concrete rolled to my feet.

"What are you doing?" George asked.

Something black sprouted between the rusted bars and broken planks.

"Meggie, stop!"

I kept pounding. Under the flashlight beam, I could see bumpy shapes. The bench was hollow. Dirt and leaves sifted from the chinks. A sour odor opened, like a musty flower. My mouth filled with saliva. There was a strange rustling noise from inside the bench, and to my astonishment, a stream of black poured to my feet. I let out a shriek.

On the ground lay clumps of earth with twigs poking out. I looked closer. They were small bird carcasses, one on top of another. George bent down and touched a bird. It rolled off with a dry crackle. "Bloody hell," he said, and ran a hand over the twisted shapes.

I picked one up. Its threadlike legs were pulled tight to a shrunken belly, neck out. My fingers groped for another, then another. Their heads and beaks were fully formed, but their wings were stunted. About a dozen had stayed whole; the rest were a silted mound of bones and feathers.

"Meggie, let's go," Aunt Inez said.

I pushed my fingers into the ground. The smell of dust and rot was overpowering.

My aunt stood above me. "Meggie, you know what to do. A dead baby bird is the same as a lost child."

I stayed on the ground.

"If we don't bury them, they'll come back to haunt us. And then we must shout their names."

She brought me a few flat stones and dug a good-sized hole, her fingers working in fast strokes; then she dropped handfuls of birds inside. I covered them with a layer of dirt. Uncle Tom kept watch over my father, who was sitting up now.

George swung his beam inside the ripped-open bench. "The damn thing's dry as a tinderbox. That's why they kept like that."

Inside the bench were more birds, covered by twigs and leaves. They looked beautiful, with their half-opened beaks and cracked wings. I carried them to my aunt and we kept digging.

"I figured out what happened," George called out. "There's a hole right here at the top. The mother bird must have kept laying her eggs in the bench for her nest. The bench was too tall for the baby birds to fly from. Each year she returned, built a nest on top of the old ones, and crushed the children who came before."

"George, help us out here," my aunt ordered.

My cousin squatted next to me and we dug. Clumps of grass tore like hair in my hands. I sprinkled dirt over the broken shapes, arranged grass on top. When I finished, the ground looked like a furrowed field.

My aunt's silhouette was sharp against the sky. In her palms she held a bird, its beak opened so wide it might swallow an egg. She placed the bird in my waiting hands and pointed to my father.

He did not even blink as I laid the bird at his feet. I shut my eyes, waited for some sign from him. Then I felt his touch, cool as water, on my cheek. My eyes stirred open. His fingers pointed at the ground.

The hole I dug was long and steep. The bird rested on its side, head poised on a long, skinny neck, as if it was trying to keep its mouth aboveground. With each clod that I threw, the carcass trembled.

When I looked up, I saw anger brooding on my father's forehead, pinning me there.

Let me go, I begged.

His face did not change. I began to run, the grass slippery as ice under my feet.

"Go!" I cried. My family watched as I circled around and around the bench. An awful quiet fell upon us. I tried calling his name, but my throat was empty.

In the morning the house was polished with order. My father's belongings were stacked in the corridor. He was asleep in Timmy's bedroom, the door kept shut. A lot had been arranged, though I didn't know the details.

For me there was only the rubble of memory, a dead baby bird in my aunt's palms, my father pitching himself off the hill. The ruined bench. There was no answer, just parents leading their children to death. A patter started in my mind. *Tell me who I am. Tell me who I am without my father.*

"Sheila and I are taking you out," my mother announced after supper. I followed her as she danced up the stairs, humming under her breath, her movements tiny and preoccupied. She foraged in the armoire, then put on a blue-flowered dress, and a gauzy blue scarf around her neck.

"Where are we going?" I asked.

"To the fair. We have a lot to talk about."

From the back of the armoire my mother brought out some of my clothes—a maroon jersey that hugged my waist. I recognized it as one of the items we'd bought the summer before, on our shopping spree. I put on the rest of what she'd chosen. A short kilt skirt flared at my thighs; my legs were sheathed in matching tights. My hair swung to my shoulders, black and glossy. When I looked in the mirror, I felt snug, put together.

My mother drew me near. "When I think of how brave and stubborn you are, Meggie, how fierce you've always been, helping him all these years, it's amazing."

I turned my face away. "I'm not. I'm none of those things."

"Yes you are. You're the most stubborn person I know."

"Your mother is right," Sheila put in. "I see that fire in your eyes."

I touched the scar on my chin. It was a needle-thin crescent, ridged by a darker purple. She caught my hand. "No, you misunderstand. Your father, he was a dreamer. You burn with the real thing. That's why he got afraid. He believed you going to steal his passion and go farther than him."

"It's not true. I disappointed him." *I almost walked into the fire,* I wanted to add. *I'm the same as he.*

We set out for the fair, my mother on one side of me, Sheila on the other. I tried to memorize the swing of their arms, the bounce of their gaits. *I am with the women now,* I told myself, as we hiked through the woods, the dirt path smooth under our feet. *I am not with that silent man and his books.*

At the fair, as we strolled down the aisles of booths, the music whipped into a tight, intense beat. We tried a game of darts and failed miserably. The pointed tips rebounded off the wooden edge of the target instead of piercing the bright balloons. Laughing, we shifted to another stall and bought a bag of taffy.

Then I felt a hand on my arm. "Megan." My mother's lips trembled. They were the inside blush of a rose. "Listen, darling, we've made some decisions about school for you." A square of green fluttered from her fist as she let go of a taffy wrapper. "After all, September is around the bend."

"What does that mean?"

Now Sheila spoke. "The question is, Should you stay here in England or go back to the States?"

"What are you talking about? I'm staying with you," I told my mother. I stuffed a piece of taffy into my mouth. She exchanged glances with Sheila. "Isn't that right?"

"Your father has to stay here. I can't be far away."

My mother lifted her face to the sky. A huge round shadow slanted across our path. Sheila and I also looked up. The Ferris wheel spun, seemed to topple on its spindle. Each time the black wheel swept up again, children's high-pitched screams flowed into the air.

"I have an idea," my mother said. "Let's do that." Before I could object, she had run to the booth, bought tickets, and returned to stand on line with us. As we inched forward, the wheel kept sweeping up and around.

"Sheila has made some inquiries through friends of hers," she continued. "There's a very nice boarding school in Massachusetts. It's just for a year. I talked to them, and your high school is sending your records. They were so impressed with how advanced you are, they may take you as a junior."

Her words bounced off me, like the darts clattering off the wooden target.

"Putting you in school in England doesn't make sense," she went on. "It's a different system. At fifteen they're getting ready for their comprehensives to go to university. You do understand, don't you?"

You don't understand. I don't know who I am. Tell me who I am.

"I know it's awful," Sheila said, "with everything you've been through, Meggie. That's why it's better you get some time away. Imagine, one year at a fancy school. And you so pretty! Think of all the boyfriends that will line up outside your door!"

When my mother tried to put her arms around me, I tore them off. "No!" I shouted. "I can't leave!" Wildly I glanced around, half expecting to see Ron Cone jump out of a shiny black car by the candied-apple stand.

"Your turn, ladies!" someone barked. Fingers and elbows prodded me forward, and we were guided onto a platform and eased into a seat. My mother's treacherous softness, her perfume settled on my hair and arms. I pressed down into the seat, breathed its heavy metallic smell. No. I belonged in a closed room. With him.

The iron bar fell, clanging, to our laps. A moment later, I saw that Sheila had remained behind. She waved to us. "That's it, Meggie!" she called out. "It's going to be all right, darling!"

A metal noise ripped beneath our bottoms and we swayed backward into the air. The wheel stopped so a family could climb on, then lurched up a few more feet, stopped again. Two more families boarded and we jerked upward.

"Look how far we can see!" my mother exclaimed.

My throat was shut. Below, the stalls and tents were dollhouse-sized. I saw my mother's white knuckles grip the bar. Her laughs became little gasps. She tossed her scarf over her shoulder. It blew to the side, then draped over our faces. We both

were tangled in a sheet of tear-stained blue. My mother grabbed
at the material, smoothed it around her neck.

"Why are you doing this to me?" I asked.

Her eyes were on a distant point. "I ran away to marry a
man with an idea in his head," she told me. "But there was more
than I imagined to him—his family, everything, their stories. I
just didn't know that the idea would become too big for him, too
big for all of us." She paused, then added, "We have to move on."

"Ma." I pressed myself against her. She hesitated, and put
her arm around me, her fingers resting on my sleeve. I wanted
her to save me. There was only air around us. My mother seemed
to weigh nothing.

The wheel hub groaned. In my mind, my mother struggled
up from her seat and climbed over the guard rail. Gingerly she
stepped onto the clouds, which made fluffy tufts at the backs of
her high heels.

"Where are you going?" I shouted.

"I have a job, I have a job," I thought she called back, but the
wind snatched her words and carried them off.

Then I realized my mother was showing me the way out.
She was the one who had cut off her hair to run away from
home, who flew from Guyana, blood spilling behind. She
walked, balanced high over the crater of sadness, her spine strong
and erect. I remembered what I'd heard about the bird-ghosts.
They wanted light, air. One scratch of wind and she would
bruise. She moved so effortlessly, the clouds up near her waist
now. Soon they had taken over her shoulders and she dragged a
fleecy train.

"Meggie, come!" she called.

The chair swayed as I raised myself. The sky was scarred

with my father's silence. My feet were strong and sure, guiding me out. Clouds cushioned my heels. I took another step, and another. It was true. I was born in the blood of leaving. I too needed air. Wind filled me, sweet and cool. My bones were clear glass. I flew, over Sudbury, over the black water and old curses.

The whole globe spread before me. I saw a black-and-yellow sky, chunks of continents covered in waving seas. I saw rivers divide, families scatter in a thousand directions, to the Caribbean, Africa, England, and North America. They scattered once again, sons and daughters falling off an edge, a salt-blue melancholy running through our veins. I saw our own family roost here in England, each summer discrete, time streaming between. My father was right. Particle and wave, we must try to hold fast to who we are, yet travel on. We can always return to memory, our stories stamped on our bones, shaping our mouths as we cry out in fear and love.

I cupped my hands over my lips. His name sliced deep. "Warren!" I called.

When I looked over, my mother remained beside me. The scarf twisted into the air and danced like a flame below. The Ferris wheel lurched, the ground swept up and out.

Together we began to shout, *Warren!*

A hole opened in me, and the night came rushing through. The stars gathered into a knot that scorched me clean. My father was everywhere, crouched behind the wooden booths, high above, flinging out milky bits of light. It will be like this for the rest of my life, holding on, letting go. Again and again I shouted his name, until the sky went still, and my childhood, my summers in Sudbury, tipped off the edge of the earth.

10